Bethel Manor ~ inner secrets dying to be told that may burst the welcoming façade of the manor's beautiful exterior.

Fredrick and Elizabeth Shaw, James and Clare Blackwell ~ families and faith tested to the breaking point. Is a thin veil of courtesy and decorum hiding deceit within the manor?

James's relationship with Clare's best friend Phoebe Tripp was always considered a friendship of convenience during Clare's temporary blindness. Was their dalliance more than either cared to admit? Enraged, Phoebe's husband Patrick sets out on a mission to uncover the truth and destroy two households to prove his suspicions.

Rivalry causes dissension among the household servants. A maid slated to replace the beloved head of staff spreads lies and half-truths to further divide the family.

Bethel Manor ~ can those inside survive in this latest tale of love and loyalty?

Beatrice Fishback Books

Fiction:
Bethel Manor
Bethel Manor Reborn
Dying to Eat at the Pub
Loving a Selfie
Christmas at the Corp
Winter Writerland

Non-fiction:
Loving Your Military Man
Defending the Military Marriage
Defending the Military Family

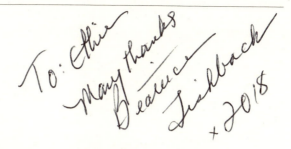

To: Ethie
Many thanks
Beatrice Fishback
× 2018

Bethel Manor Secrets

Beatrice Fishback

 Mrs. Ethie Moak
277 Verbeck Ave.
Schaghticoke, NY 12154-2718

518 3665656

ISBN: 9781717988225

ACKNOWLEDGEMENTS

To Jim: lover of my heart and exemplar father and grandfather. Thanks for your continued patience with this mercurial writer.

To wonderful critique partners: Irene Onorato, Dana K. Ray, and Linda Robinson. Once again, the words in this story would have no song without your tunes of encouragement and exhortation.

DEDICATION

To father and grandfather, Graham Woods, who was called to the gates of heaven far too soon. Bethel Manor's Fredrick Shaw demonstrates Graham's model of loving-kindness by all who knew and loved him. We are extremely grateful for Graham's life and his family.

Chapter One

**The Fens
January 1849**

Patrick Tripp paced Willow Field's flagstone floor. If anger dressed in clothing, his would be swathed in a black, mourning cape.

Servants slept in segregated quarters along the long corridor after their sixteen-hour shifts of serving the family and completing chores.

For the moment, flickering candles atop the long kitchen table were his sole companions, the surrounding silence a blessing and a curse. The large room gave ample space to traipse back and forth and release pent-up tensions.

Sleep was elusive. Being alone allowed the temptation to mull over the deception discovered in his home.

How could his wife double-cross him and allow her feelings to wander to another man?

Whenever James Blackwell's name came up, Phoebe blushed like a new bride. But neither of them knew he had uncovered their dalliances while he'd been away.

Daphne, their trustworthy housekeeper's unintentional slip during a routine conversation yesterday had solidified his suspicions. "Mister James came quite often when you were gone, sir, and kept the mistress company." She had folded the linen napkins with precision, unaware of the verbal blunder she'd committed.

"He what?" Patrick felt the heat of anger and squeezed his fists into tight balls.

"Me's sorry, sir, if me said something wrong." She had stopped the rote motion of the half and quarter-fold of fabric and hung her head. But the damage had been done. She'd confirmed what he instinctively knew.

He stopped his pacing at the east-facing window where stars in the sky scintillated alluringly as if teasing with promiscuous behavior. Had Phoebe batted her eyes at James and caused him to stumble? Or had Phoebe been the innocent one who had been taken advantage of by Patrick's friend?

James had been rejected and cast aside by his wife Clare when she had fallen ill and became blind after the birth of their son. Who wouldn't have been enraptured by the man's attention, a newborn cradled in his arms and lacking female companionship?

Did he have a part to play in Phoebe and James being drawn together? His endless excursions abroad had left his wife vulnerable and lonely.

Patrick held up a balled fist and shook it at the black-draped sky that clutched the glittering lights. Regardless of who initially enticed the other, James Blackwell would never get away with whatever had happened between him and his wife.

He snuffed out the candles with a pinch of two fingers and left the kitchen. Phoebe had asked they share her room this evening but he had feigned tiredness. What he wanted to do was shout out his pain at her deceit.

Patrick labored up the wide circular stairs leading to the upper rooms as if the weight of the heavens rested on his shoulders.

Cold, night air infiltrated his bedroom, and he shuddered as he disrobed and slipped into bed. Tomorrow would begin his quest towards seeking revenge.

+ + +

Howling winds encircled Bethel Manor. Like an unruly wraith, a current of air whipped through crevices and down chimney pots, causing the flames in the hearth below to wave back and forth from its intrusion.

Clare Blackwell wrapped her shawl tighter. She strode past one box to another and supervised the staff as they handled delicate glass-blown baubles, designed by Hans Greiner, being preserved for next year.

Christmas was over, the festivities nearly forgotten, and the mundane chore of putting the ornaments away had begun.

Storing the extra candles and decorations in a dry place was hopelessly boring and a ghastly reminder of the months of dark, dreary days ahead. They would go by as if a woolen blanket had been thrust over the earth and its residents barely finding enough habitable air to share.

"It's always distressing to observe the end of celebrations."

"I know it is, my dear." Elizabeth, James's mother sat on a thick throw rug covered with a blanket beside George Andrew who cooed with contentment. "But it's time the tree came down and things put away." She shook a wooden rattle over the child who shrieked with delight.

Clare knelt beside Elizabeth and allowed her black ringlets to tickle the baby's nose. He screeched again, reached out and clutched a lock of Clare's hair with chubby fingers. She gently unrolled the fingers from their clasp and kissed his forehead. "You're such a dear. My life has been truly blessed with your presence."

"And with mine, I dare hope?" James had entered the formal dining room, more often used for special guests than wrapping and storing items.

Clare rose and kissed his cheek. "How would I *have* George if it weren't for you?" She whispered sultrily in his ear.

James's blush ran up his thin neck, along his narrow cheeks and across his temple. Each day Clare's eyesight improved, and she was eternally grateful for the ability to see expressions on her husband's face.

She pouted at the now-filled containers. "Don't you loathe this must be done?"

"Is it truly such hard work?"

Clare picked up a shiny globe-shaped ornament and spun it gently. Refracted light glittered off oak walls creating a rainbow effect. George followed the mesmerizing motion with his eyes and giggled, his legs pumping with delight.

"It's not difficult. It just makes me sad the holidays are finished and there's little to look forward to."

"Then what I have to say should sound appealing." James's lanky frame drew near and he gazed on Clare with the adoration she recalled from the first days they'd declared their love for each other five years before. What would her life have been like without him? Because of her illness and subsequent blindness, she had allowed herself to pull away from this delightful man and nearly lost him forever. It would never happen again.

Clare perched on tiptoe and replaced the

drooping curl along James's forehead back into place. "What is it?"

"Now, now. Don't be in such a hurry. Savor surprises. Think of it as opening another Christmas gift." Glister in his green eyes testified to his mischievous nature.

"You tease, James." Clare smiled. "You know how much I rush through unwrapping gifts in anticipation of what's next. My patience is limited." She dropped from her tiptoes.

"How well I know." James chuckled.

"What is it?"

"Shall I tell her, dear Mother?" James dropped to one knee beside George.

"You mustn't goad her on." Elizabeth pushed herself up as James lifted the infant, handed him to Clare, and took the ornament she'd been handling and placed it inside the last box.

"What do you think about a small—"

"Yes? Tell me." Clare cradled her child and bounced slightly to stop his whimpering.

"Something to cheer you up." James caressed their baby's cheek with the back of his hand. "Shush, little one."

George Andrew cooed at his father's touch, closed his eyes and grew heavy in Clare's arms.

Clare softened her tone. "Please. Don't keep me in suspense any longer."

"What would your opinion be about a

small holiday?"

She squealed and George wiggled. Clare whispered, "Where? Where shall we go? Father and Elizabeth should accompany us, as well."

"Most assuredly."

"And your sister, Grace, would do well with a trip after losing Braedyn to that dreadful murderer." Clare grew solemn.

"Your father and I have already spoken about it and everyone will travel together. Sam's much better since his cart accident and is perfectly capable of taking care of the estate while we're away."

"It's settled then?" Clare smiled, kissed George's forehead and brought him tighter to her chest.

"All settled."

"This news makes putting everything away a little easier. Thank you, dearest."

"You have your father to thank. He sensed everyone was a tad downtrodden with Christmas ending."

"He's such a thoughtful man." Ruby red hue flashed across Elizabeth's cheeks.

"A life could not be any more blessed than mine." Clare nodded approval as the last box was closed. "I should never complain about one wonderful season ending. Instead, I should anticipate the next season and what adventure awaits us."

"An adventure we shall have." James

drew George's blanket tighter and kissed the child's exposed fingers. "All of us."

Chapter Two

Clare held a cobalt blue taffeta dress against her waist and rubbed the dress sleeve slowly along her jawline. Its fine, luxurious silk was soft as George Andrew's skin.

She strutted in front of the cheval mirror, with its mahogany frame, as if she were Queen Victoria in a parade. Clare cupped her palm in a small wave and smiled at the royal rendition. Queen Victoria was held in high regard, and their country had earned deep respect throughout the world because of her leadership, along with Prime Minister Lord John Russell. Clare was extremely proud of her heritage.

She replaced the dress in the wardrobe. Sadly, its light fabric would never do for a winter outing.

"What else is there for me to choose from?" Clare asked Abigail, who had recently become her personal maid. Abigail assisted with

Clare's clothing, performed secretarial duties when the need arose, and often dressed her when a special event warranted help. But the girl was young and, on several occasions, had muddled what she had been directed to do.

Clare's wardrobe must be perfect for their upcoming trip. Last time she had ventured on an expedition was before she and James married, or had even declared their love. It was a time when her father had been persistently stubborn and insisted she not venture from Bethel Manor. She had snuck away with her best friend, Phoebe, and her family on a ship to Brugge. But Father's sudden illness had taken her back to the estate in a flurry of fear and contrition. She hadn't been away since.

She scrutinized her reflection. How many times had she deeply hurt people she loved? James and Father tolerated her outbursts of pride and selfishness with grace and decorum. But God had been touching her heart, urging her to shed the natural clothing of selfishness she tended to wear and to put on a heart of compassion and kindness instead.

Abigail presented a deep green-colored shawl. "Would this cashmere be useful, miss?"

Clare turned. "Why it's perfect. Well done."

The young maid blushed. "May I also suggest the sable muff? I do believe it would be most helpful."

"I'd forgotten about the muff. You're such a clever girl."

"Thank you, milady." Abigail placed Clare's things on the bed. A journey could take weeks to prepare for, yet Father and James had only given them a few days.

"Are you excited to accompany me on this trip?" Clare folded other garments into a neat stack and placed them next to the shawl and muff.

"I'm afraid I won't be coming." Abigail's mouth formed a thin line and her eyes hardened, but her tone remained even. "I've been told there will be servants to assist you when you arrive at your destination."

Clare touched Abigail's forearm. "Oh, dear. I'm dreadfully sorry. I assumed you'd be traveling with me. But this opportunity will give you time to visit with your family in Bury St. Edmunds. I know you aren't able to see them often."

"No, milady. I won't be able to leave." Abigail's cheeks tightened.

"What a shame." Clare turned back to the mirror and spoke to the maid's reflection. "Let me speak to Father and see if he would make an exception for you."

The young girl brightened. "I'd be very pleased if you could, miss."

"I see no reason why you shouldn't have a few days to yourself and enjoy time with your parents."

Abigail curtsied and left.

Clare rearranged the clothing and sat on the chaise lounge in the corner and rummaged through treasured pieces of jewelry given by her mother years before her death.

Rap. Rap.

"Come in." Clare stood. "Did you forget something, Abigail?"

"It's me." Father, tall and dignified, did not show his years. In fact, since he had married Elizabeth, he appeared to have grown younger. Their love was a touching testimony of two lonely people who had discovered each other through God's providence. Who would ever imagine God would bring James's mother and her father together? It was indeed a match made in heaven. "I'm not disturbing you, am I?"

"Of course not. Oh, Father, I'm beyond words at your decision to take us away. Thank you from the bottom of my heart. Where are we going? James insisted you tell me yourself."

She directed him towards the chaise. "Come sit next to me. I was considering what I should take when you knocked."

Her father sat on the edge of the lounge and Clare curled up nearer the top where a tall headrest made for comfortable reclining.

"Is there anything the matter?" She sat upright and took hold of his hand. "You seem pensive."

"It's nothing, I suppose."

"Apparently something has you concerned. There're furrows alongside your eyes. You've been extremely happy these days. It appears you aren't right now. What is it?"

"I've had a long conversation with Sam about our journey."

"Is he incapable of taking care of things while we're gone?" Clare released her grip and sat upright.

"No. It's nothing like that. Sam's stronger than ever and has quite a strict regimen with the workload he's outlined, and I'm extremely impressed with the details."

"What could it be?"

"He mentioned potential dissatisfaction with younger staff. Sam and I belong to the old school when servants never questioned desires of the master of the house."

She grabbed his hands again and squeezed. "How could they be unhappy with you? Everyone agrees you're the best landowner countywide."

"Obviously I'm not handling particular issues to their liking."

"Such as?"

"Such as who can go to their respective families while we're gone."

"Oh, dear." Clare rose.

"It seems you've heard this as well?"

"Abigail mentioned her wishes to me

before you came. I told her I would ask you to make an exception in her case."

Her father rose. "If I say yes to one, others may be upset if they aren't allowed. How can I give in to her and not cause envy with the rest? Surely you can see my dilemma."

"I hadn't considered how it would affect an entire household."

"I'm sure Sam could take care of Bethel Manor with fewer workers, but how would I decide who should go? I believe it's best everyone stays and continue with their duties. When we get back, I'll create a rota and allow each member several days off."

"Seems a generous proposal. I feel dreadful I gave Abigail hope I'd try and obtain permission from you though."

"You'll have to inform her no one is allowed special treatment."

Clare sat on the chaise's edge. "Must I? We've just begun to have a rapport. To trust each other."

"I'm sorry. Abigail must be told."

"She won't take the news well."

"You can tell her everyone can expect a holiday on our return. Hopefully, she'll be satisfied with that option."

She rose. "You're such a dear man. I'm sure the servants will understand the necessity of waiting."

"I hope you're right, my dear." Father,

shoulders curled forward, exited.

Clare stepped to the window and watched below as he headed out the front door. He stopped and chatted with Sam and two other male servants. The ramrod, younger men nodded. No expressions on their faces.

Father looked up, a frown crossing his face, and shook his head. Being master of an estate came with its joy and challenges, and apparently, he had just encountered one of those challenges.

Chapter Three

Fredrick rearranged a small, pink tufted chair closer to the inglenook fireplace, sat and raised his palms to the heat. "The house activity is quite tiring."

Elizabeth lowered her copy of *Jane Eyre*. "I thought you were looking forward to our excursion. You've been hush-hush about it, perhaps keeping secrets is becoming too much."

She tilted her head. Reflections from the blaze shone along her flowing tresses and resembled the splendor of grain fields shimmering in evening light.

Fredrick resisted an urge to rush to Elizabeth's side, intertwine fingertips in her hair and kiss her passionately.

His first wife, Florence, had blessed him with his beautiful daughter Clare. When Florence died, he'd been devastated for many years.

Yet God restored his life with this woman who now sat before him. There were times his love for Elizabeth was more than he could bear, and tenderness in his spirit welled up in unabashed tears.

"Are you all right?" Elizabeth shifted as if to rise.

He patted the air. "Please don't get up. Everything's fine. I don't want you to worry about me."

"Shall I read to you?" She picked up the book. "Since Clare taught me how to read, I can't get enough. Charlotte Brontë is such an inspiration."

"How so?" Fredrick rubbed the top of his thighs with now-warmed hands.

"Did you know Miss Brontë was sent to the Clergy Daughter's School in Lancashire after her mother passed away? Two of her sisters died from tuberculosis because of the horrendous conditions in the school." Elizabeth held the book higher. "Lowood is part of the setting in this novel and was based on experiences in Lancashire."

"I'm pleased you're enjoying it." Fredrick rose and walked the perimeter of the room, stopped again in front of the fire and gazed at the gyrating flames.

Elizabeth set the book on the chaise and joined him. "What is it, my darling?"

"There's an unsettled air within the staff. I

tried to cajole them with promises of what to expect on our return from holiday, yet someone seems to have stirred a hornet's nest in their midst, and tensions in their quarters is quite strained."

"Are you sure you aren't being overly concerned?"

He caressed her hair with a cupped hand. "You always make me feel better whenever we speak. What would I do without you?'

"You would handle the situation as deemed best. I'm sure you will sort everything. You're the most wonderful landowner I know."

Fredrick moved nearer the window. The darkness was thick, and a cloud covering dipped so low it was impossible to see even the faintest movement. Early evenings could create a sense of warmth or of suffocation. He pressed his forehead into the glass. "Clare said the same thing. Yet I've never had this feeling of unease before. It makes me hesitant to leave."

"You've been looking forward to this time away, but we can delay our departure if you think it's necessary."

He spun around. "I won't change our plans because of someone's childish behavior. I could understand if a parent was unwell and they needed to return home. But I'm unaware of any such issues."

Elizabeth joined him and gently held his arm. The muscle under his jacket flexed at her touch. "Let's chat about our trip. We can write a list of things we may have forgotten to pack and take your mind off this matter."

Fredrick kissed her forehead and lingered for a moment. "I'm so grateful for you."

She drew close and leaned on his chest. "And I, you."

They strolled back to the settee and sat side-by-side. The warmth of Elizabeth's nearness soothed any apprehension. Perhaps he was overreacting. Above everything else, he wanted nothing more than for this to be a journey they would remember for a lifetime.

+ + +

"How many bags must a woman bring?" James teased Clare who was surrounded by a stack of hatboxes, three small crates and two travel trunks in her adjoining bedroom.

"Do you suppose it's too much?" She collapsed on one of the trunks. "George needs many essentials. We may have to hire extra carriages to carry everything."

"I haven't seen you this excited since you found out you were with child." He crouched before Clare and placed a hand on her knee. "Speaking of being with child. We've said we'd like to consider a brother or sister for George. Do you think it's too soon? You had such difficulty with his birth. I'd hate for you to go through anything similar again. I couldn't bear it."

She touched his face. Her dark eyes

floated in a pool and would it be possible, he'd dive in and swim for eternity. "You won't lose me. And I'd do anything to please you."

How had he managed to be loved by someone like her? He, an orphan. She, a maiden of fairest beauty. His roots went no deeper than a poor man's pocket. Hers were wealth and status. The one thing they had in common was a deep faith in a forgiving and loving God.

He rose and gently pulled her up. "You'd take the chance to become ill again for me? For us?"

"We can't allow George to grow up without a playmate, can we?" The bewitching twinkling in her eyes drew him close.

He bent to reach her diminutive stature and their lips touched slightly.

"After all, he'll want a brother to lord it over, don't you agree?" She spoke the words into his mouth with a warm breath.

James gulped. "I'm certain of it." He clasped her into a tight embrace and snuggled his face into the thick, black tresses spiraling over her shoulders. "I love you, Clare. I'm thankful God saw fit to heal you."

"And healed our marriage." She murmured.

"Yes, and our marriage." He released her slightly, afraid she would break like a piece of fine porcelain if he clasped any tighter.

Clare stepped back. "I suppose we should

finish our packing. Father wants the bags ready when the carriages arrive first thing tomorrow. But I promise. You'll hold another child in your arms soon enough." She winked.

If only he could be as confident as Clare about bringing children into the world. It seemed to be changing at a faster pace than he ever imagined. An underwater tunnel bored beneath the River Thames would have been unheard of ten years ago and it was an engineering feat he longed to see.

On the other hand, word of a great famine in Ireland forcing millions to flee could surely be overcome with the ingenuity found in those who created the London masterpiece. Yet again, political turmoil gurgled like boiling mud pits. What would it be like to subject children to a life of such unknowns?

"James? Is everything okay?" Clare's voice snapped him from his reverie.

"Um. Yes. Of course."

Rap. Rap.

"Come in," Clare said.

Abigail curtsied, deep pursed lines along her lips. "Excuse me, milady, Mister James has a visitor."

"I do?" James gave a side-glance to Clare. "Now who could it possibly be? I wasn't expecting anyone today."

"It's a Mister Patrick Tripp, sir."

"Patrick? How delightful."

"Before you leave, Abigail, please forgive me for making a promise I couldn't keep," Clare said.

"What's this about?" James paused.

"I told Abigail I would speak to Father about her visiting her family while we were away. I was unaware no one would be allowed to leave."

"Surely Fredrick has a reason for this decision."

Abigail lowered her eyes, her tone harsh. "I'm sure he does, sir. No need to worry, milady. I understand you had no part in this."

"Thank you."

"May I leave now?" Abigail asked.

"By all means." Worry lines spread across Clare's forehead.

"We shall discuss this later. I must go and see Patrick."

Abigail exited and James followed. It had been ages since he had seen his friend, and they had much to catch up on.

Chapter Four

Patrick overlooked Bethel Manor's rear garden through the sitting room's frosted windowpane. Winter's frozen breath had blown crystals along hedgerows and flattened fields to a frozen, barren plain. Her stay seemed to have lasted an eternity.

The ride from Willow Field had given him plenty of time to carefully consider what to say. Dare he confront James or wait and let him speak for himself? Was it wise to be here with this fury of jealousy? Hearing of Phoebe's behavior caused an anger he'd never known before, and it frightened him. His stomach cramped and his jaw clenched tightly. Other times, it was as if someone punched him. The distress made his whole body palpitate with pain.

He shifted his cravat and swallowed. Childish tears would not be tolerated. He was a gentleman and would behave accordingly.

"My dear friend. How wonderful to see you." James strode in, his long legs and thin arms seemed to move with the ease of a nimble branch swayed by a breeze. Casual. Self-controlled.

Patrick's cravat strangled him further and he pulled on it once more.

James patted his back. "Dearest Patrick. Are you home for a while?"

"Yes. There'll no longer be any extended trips, I can assure you." Could James not see the beast struggling within? Perhaps he was a better thespian than he imagined.

"How's Phoebe? And your children?"

How dare he speak his wife's name with such an intimate tone? "They're well. And Sara and Daniel are both growing."

"There's no doubt, I won't recognize them next time we meet."

Patrick shifted from one leg to the next and clasped his hands behind his back. "How's Clare? I'm sorry for what she went through after George was born."

"That's in the past. I'm pleased to say, she's doing extremely well. She'll join us shortly as she wanted to see you for herself. Please sit." With a blithe movement, James pointed to a chair, sat on the settee and stretched out his legs.

Patrick took the chair nearest the fire, altered its direction and faced James. "I'm pleased to hear it. It was quite a difficult time for everyone."

"Indeed. Doctor Willard wasn't convinced she'd regain her sight. God saw fit to restore everything, however."

"How wonderful for you." A spasm along Patrick's right arm jerked and he rubbed the aching muscle.

James sat upright. "Are you certain everything's all right?"

"Why wouldn't I be?"

"I've no idea. You seem tense. As if something's bothering you."

"Why should anything be wrong? Is there something you know you're not telling me?"

"No. I can't think of anything. Tell me, how are your parents? I'm sure they miss you terribly." James shifted and yanked at a pant leg.

"You've no idea how much they long for their grandchildren."

"Dearest Patrick, how wonderful to see you." Clare floated in like a small bird with her ebony hair and lively eyes, her translucent skin a striking contrast to a dark shawl draped over her shoulders.

"And you, Clare. You look simply stunning." He rose and took her hand. Did she have any idea what a fiend of a husband she had? Surely she wouldn't be this beautifully serene if she knew of his treacherous conduct.

"Why thank you. How very kind."

James stood and encircled her waist with his arm. "She's exquisite, is she not?"

Clare batted her eyelashes at James. "Why, sir, you embarrass me with your charms."

They giggled like two schoolchildren, as if unaware Patrick was directly in front of them.

"Don't mind us. We're merely flirting with one another." James brushed Clare's cheek with his lips and his gesture left a blush of crimson.

"That behavior is allowed with one's *own* wife." Patrick picked up his cap. "I must go." If he didn't leave, what he was about to say may forever damage this household, and he wasn't sure he was ready to speak his mind.

"Must you?" Clare stepped up to him. "Why you've only just arrived."

"I'm sorry. I've forgotten something urgent at home needing my immediate attention." He grabbed his overcoat and hurried out to the foyer. Donning his coat and hat, he opened the front door and exited. A winter day never felt this numbingly cold.

+ + +

"What was that about?" James strode to the closed door.

"I'm not sure, Patrick's definitely not himself. Perhaps he has something on his mind and wasn't sure whether to share what burdened him."

He turned towards her. "But why come this distance and leave without saying anything? Do you think I should go after him?"

"I'm not sure it would do any good. It was as if he were suffering somehow."

"Suffering?"

"An inner pain. I recognized the look. Even when I didn't have sight, I knew when I sat at my dressing table my reflection showed the anguish in my soul. It's what I saw in Patrick."

James grabbed her hands and clasped them. "I'm sorry you were in such agony. What do you suppose is causing such angst in Patrick?"

"I've no idea. If I had to guess he's struggling about something, a betrayal perhaps, or maybe someone he loves is experiencing affliction. I hope it's nothing to do with Phoebe. Could it be one of their parents?"

"When I mentioned his parents, he didn't elaborate." He released her hands.

"I'll send a note to Phoebe and inquire if everything's all right with the family."

"Bear in mind we leave tomorrow for our journey."

"Ah, yes. Now I wonder if we shouldn't forgo our trip just for a short time depending on what I hear back." Clare nibbled a thumbnail.

"Phoebe wouldn't listen to any such nonsense. She'd want you to go and enjoy your family and make memories, don't you think?"

"Yes, she would."

"But I'm sure she'd greatly appreciate a note and suggest we visit upon our return."

"I'll go directly to pen a letter." Clare disappeared out the door and up the stairway.

He moved to the window. Patrick seemed like a man tormented by a demon. He didn't want to alarm Clare there was more to what was going on than James was willing to admit.

Patrick looked at him as if peering at an enemy, a soldier ready to do battle and not willing to let down his armor. There would be more visits from Patrick in the future and ones not filled with pleasantries. Of that, he was certain.

Chapter Five

James entered the foyer. Sweet aromas filtered from the dining room. Preparations were obviously being made for the midday meal.

On any other occasion, scents of venison and vegetables made his mouth water. Roast potatoes and steamed cabbage served in generous portions would also be on offer. Right now, his senses were repelled by any thought of food.

Patrick had shared his trips abroad would no longer happen. What did he infer by his comment? It wasn't the words as much as Patrick's tone of voice that raised hair on the back of James's neck.

"Whoa!" Fredrick cried out. He clasped the falling stack of binders to keep them from toppling.

"Forgive me, sir. I wasn't watching where I was going."

"You were in deep thought."

"Indeed."

"Is everything all right?"

"Of course."

"You look as if you've seen a ghost, my friend." Fredrick placed his binders on the center table taking up a substantial portion of the area. In spring, a large bouquet of fresh flowers would decorate the table. Right now, holly boughs from the garden neatly arranged in a bowl, filled the space.

"Perhaps a spectral from my past is coming back to haunt me."

"What could you possibly mean?"

"Patrick was here."

"And why should his visit be any cause for concern?"

"He stayed briefly, his mannerisms, the way he regarded me was alarming."

"Are you sure you aren't overreacting? Everyone seems on edge. The servants. Sam. I've even caught myself experiencing a bit of anxiety."

"I only wish I were overreacting. Patrick's eyes carried hatred. As if he could've killed me with the harshness harbored within his soul."

"How unlike him." Fredrick adjusted the wayward papers into a neat stack.

"Not if he has heard…"

"Heard what?"

"Of my visits to Phoebe last year during

his excursions."

"I always supposed Phoebe told him. Or you had shared with him."

"I had intended to. Somehow the opportunity never arose. He was gone so much, and Phoebe and I had settled between us our times together were merely to console each other in our loneliness and nothing more. As far as we're concerned, everything was forgiven and forgotten."

"Oh, dear. Have you mentioned your concerns about Patrick to Clare?"

"No. I wasn't sure what was bothering him. However, the longer I think about it the more convinced I am that's what it is."

"What do you intend to do?"

"I'm not sure."

"You'll work something out. In the meantime, I must take care of these before we go." Fredrick picked up the now rearranged binders and cradled them in his arms. "The last thing I need to do is give Sam unfinished business. He already has his hands full with the servant's demands."

"Sam is perfectly capable of handling whatever you deem necessary to leave in his care. This trip will do everyone some good. I'm looking forward to our time away."

"I wish I could be at peace about it." Fredrick headed in the direction of his office.

James's admiration of his father-in-law

ran deep. The load the man carried in his arms seemed light compared to the burdens of managing an estate as vast as Bethel Manor. It would take a lifetime for him to learn half of what was needed to follow in Fredrick's footsteps someday.

+ + +

"Do you really think so?" Clare couldn't decide whether to allow the envy of the past to reassert itself or ignore the situation entirely in hopes it would resolve on its own. It appeared her initial instinct about Patrick being betrayed was, after all, the most compelling reason for his actions. It wasn't his words as much as the hurt etched with precision along his jawline, resembling a stone statue in a park that gave away his pain.

"I'm afraid so." James bounced George in his arms and gently patted his back. "Hush, sweet boy. Hush."

"I had concerns this might be the cause of his behavior. Don't ask me why." She placed a rattle in the crib.

"I think I should go to Willow Field and ask Patrick directly. It's the only way to find out. If it's something else, we can address whatever's going on."

"Is there time? The sun sets shortly and the paths are treacherous after dark."

"If I leave straight away, I should have plenty of time to get back without worry."

"And what will you say?"

"Ask his forgiveness, as I did you and Phoebe."

Clare paused at the cradle, her back to James. "Does Patrick have reason to be concerned for more than indiscreet visits?" She spoke softly and prodded not knowing whether she was convinced she wanted the answer.

"No, my dear." James came by her side. "But you have every right to ask."

"I hope he receives your apology and they can move on with their lives." She expelled a low sigh and faced him. "Maybe someday we can become friends with them again."

"This is my fault." James kissed George's forehead. When he looked up, tears glistened in the corner of his eyes.

"There are four people involved with this, James. I'm as guilty as you. And Patrick, if he's honest, will see his own part in leaving Phoebe with two small children on many seemingly unnecessary occasions."

"I must take full responsibility."

"Then do so. Once you've spoken to Patrick, it's up to him on whether to forgive or harden his heart."

"If only it were so simple."

"It isn't simple. It takes time to rebuild trust. Our going away will probably be for the best. Patrick will have time to consider whether to move on or stay put in his anger. Anger serves no purpose and I pray he forgives you."

Clare took George, now fast asleep, and laid him in the crib. His tranquil manner was to be admired, a trait adults would do well to bear in mind. Peace in life was much more appealing than rage. When hostility was allowed to reign, everyone suffered. The one who held the hatred suffered the most. If only Patrick could find his peace with James and move on with his life with Phoebe and their children. She prayed it would be so. She draped a blanket over her little boy's body and caressed his back until he settled once more.

Chapter Six

Was it uncertainty or deep-rooted fear causing Phoebe's arms to tingle with tiny bumps? "What do you mean you went to Bethel Manor?"

"I went to *confront* James."

"About what?"

Fireplaces were being attended to in every room of Willow Field. Even so, a chill caused Phoebe to trembled at Patrick's insinuation.

"You know precisely why I went there." Patrick circled like a tiger considering its prey.

"What did…you say?" She followed him with her eyes, afraid to breathe too deeply and set the animal within him loose.

"When Clare entered the parlor, I couldn't bring myself to speak." He stopped his pacing. "I left directly thereafter."

Phoebe conjured up a tiny bit of courage and jutted out her chin. "And what would you have said to James if you had the opportunity?"

"If I thought a dual would solve the issue, I would've challenged him right then and there."

"You wouldn't dare."

"As you wouldn't dare to be disloyal?"

"Please lower your voice. You'll wake the children." Phoebe reached out to her husband. "There was no betrayal. On either part."

Patrick shifted with a jolt as if a spark from the open flames caught hold of his coat's edge. "What would you call it?"

"Misguided conduct inappropriate to someone with an over active imagination."

"Such as Daphne and the other servants who observed this behavior?"

"So she's the one who's gossiped untruths?"

"You would deny it?"

"I would say I was lonely."

"Ah, you admit it."

"I admit to nothing except a lack of discretion around the staff. For that I am sorry. I assure you, we did not cross any unacceptable boundaries."

"What did go on while James was here during those times?" Patrick began to circle once more, closer, his eyes ablaze.

"Played games. Marbles. Cards." She placed closed fists on her hips. "We kept each other company those days and weeks while you were away."

"So this is my fault?" He stopped. The burning in his eyes softened into grief. Hurt, as if she'd slapped him, creased his cheek.

"I'm not inferring any such thing."

"What are you saying?" He rubbed his eyes with a downward motion. "I trusted you. And a man I considered a friend."

"I'm sorry, Patrick. Truly. It was never anyone's intention to cause you harm."

"Excuse me, miss, sir." Their lanky, dark-suited servant had entered.

"What is it, Arthur?" Patrick said.

"Mister James Blackwell is here to see you."

Patrick swung around to Phoebe. "Perhaps offering a dual isn't finished after all." He stomped out of the room.

+ + +

"Please give me a chance to explain," James shrugged snow off his arms and handed his overcoat to Arthur.

Patrick marched up to James with the force of a general to a troop and shoved him. "Leave my house right this minute. I believe you've already spent more time here than you should have."

"*Wait.*"

"How dare you come to my home?"

"I've come to say I'm sorry. To do whatever I can to make it up to you. To explain."

"There's no explanation necessary.

You've done enough as it is."

Phoebe rushed into the chilled foyer and grabbed her husband's raised arm. "Will you please listen to reason?"

He shoved her away. "There's no reason to hear either of you."

"We've done nothing worthy of this treatment." James held up his hands between Patrick and Phoebe. "Yes, we should have mentioned my visits to you. I admit to being lonely and—"

"And you used my wife to assuage your loneliness."

James lowered his hands and head. "Yes."

Patrick punched James's middle. "Get out. I never want to see you again." Patrick headed up the stairs, stopped at the landing and shouted. "I'll ruin you for smearing my name and destroying my family." He spun around and disappeared from view.

"I'm sorry, Phoebe." James had doubled over in anguish. He straightened and held his stomach.

"Please, don't. We were both aware we should have been more diligent in maintaining a correct decorum. It's too late now." She gazed at the empty place where her husband had been a few minutes before. "I'm not sure he'll ever forgive me. And I think it's best you leave and not return."

James retrieved and donned his overcoat.

The ache in his stomach dulled in comparison to the torture in his heart. He had never meant to cause injury to his friends. With discomfort in his body and suffering in his soul, he stepped out into the wintry night and mounted Sentra.

Darkened clouds had rolled in. A storm was eminent. James clucked his tongue to hurry the horse. Between the wintry blast of air and threatening sky of snow, he needed to return to Bethel Manor quickly.

+ + +

Clare closed the drapes. James should have returned by now. "I'm worried. What if James doesn't get back before sunset?"

Elizabeth tied off a knot on her sewing.

"He's perfectly capable of riding in difficult conditions, let's pray he returns soon." Her father, sitting at the writing desk in the far corner, stopped penning a note and glanced up.

"You're as worried as I am, Father. I can hear it in your voice."

"I'm a silly old man who loves his family." He chuckled as if to try and ease the tensions.

"Since when have you become old?" Elizabeth placed her sewing down.

"Aches and pains I've had lately are reminders I'm not as young as I used to be. I can't keep up with the workmen, and I'm ready to call it a night long before night arrives."

"Father, you're nowhere near being

elderly."

He raised his hands in mock surrender. "I give up. I was merely using my age as an excuse." And grew somber. "I don't want anything to happen to anyone I care about ever again."

"Sadly, we can't protect everyone."

"I agree. And I can only take care of those I love as much as it's in my power to do so." Fredrick headed towards the door.

"Where are you going?" Elizabeth asked.

"To find James."

"No. Please don't leave," Clare said. "He'll make it back safely. I'm sure of it."

"Now who's fooling whom? I can tell by the way your mouth purses and the wrinkles around your eyes, you are wrought with concern."

"You know me too well. I'd have even more reason to worry should you leave."

"Please don't go, Fredrick."

"How can I argue with two women?"

"It's hopeless." Clare took his elbow and guided him to the settee next to Elizabeth. "Besides, you said it yourself, you're getting older and 'tis young men who can handle the dampness." She released a slight chuckle, and fought the urge to flee and find James herself.

Chapter Seven

"I'm afraid we'll have to postpone our trip. The weather turned dreadful last night, and the carriages won't be able to make the trek to the station." Fredrick slid back under the warm eiderdown next to Elizabeth. "The trains may not be running on schedule even if we did manage to get there."

"How sad your surprise holiday's delayed." His wife snuggled under his arm and gazed at him with affection, the shimmer in her eyes a testament of deep love.

"These things happen for a reason."

"We can at least be grateful James made it home before the weather worsened."

"His appearance was sorrowful when he arrived back. As if he'd lost his best friend."

"It seems he may have."

"How foolish. On everyone's part. James and Phoebe should've never met without others in their company. It's against every propriety. I even warned him. I can't help but think Patrick is being harsh, though. He should at least hear them out."

"We learn from our mistakes, don't we? And some lessons are harder than others."

"I've made a fair share of them myself."

"As have I. Leaving James at Alpheton Orphanage when he was an infant was one of the biggest errors of my life." She sighed deeply.

"Yet look how God worked out James's future, thereby you and I could meet." He caressed the crown of her hair and wrapped a strand around his finger.

"You're right."

"It happens every once and awhile."

Elizabeth curled her lip and smiled slightly. "Are you upset the journey won't proceed as planned?"

"No. In fact, I've been concerned about the upheaval going on around the estate. I think it's best for the time being.

"Clare will be disappointed. She was looking forward to getting away from the dreariness."

"It won't be much longer, I hope. It should soon clear, and we can be on our way. In the meantime, we can allow a few of the servants to go to their homes and help to alleviate unnecessary tensions."

"How do you decide who can go?"

Elizabeth unwrapped herself from his embrace and leaned on an elbow.

"One's with seniority will go first. After them, we'll draw straws. It's the only way to demonstrate impartiality. It seems rather childish, but I just don't want anyone to think I favor one over the other."

"It seems a fair way to handle the situation."

"You're always such an encourager." He cupped her cheek. "I suppose there's no hurry to rush and leave the warmth of our room."

"And you're a romantic." Elizabeth kissed his palm and they snuggled further under the eiderdown.

+ + +

The sidebar overflowed with hot options servants had prepared for breakfast. Clare scooped a helping of eggs and toast onto a plate. Right now, only she and James were present but others would soon join them.

"Of course I'm disappointed. And look outside. The snow will take ages to melt." She paused, a mound of bread pudding perched on the spoon. "But I'm grateful you made it home. Patrick seems determined to dismiss your apologies."

"It's worse than merely dismissing my apology."

"Whatever do you mean?"

"He punched me—"

"He what?" She dropped the serving spoon back into the bowl. Creamy froth splattered on the linen cloth beneath the dish. "You didn't say anything when you returned."

"I understand his need to thrash out at someone. At me. I deserve whatever he feels is necessary to regain his honor."

"Let's pray the two of you can resolve this issue in an amicable way."

Grace glided in. She still wore the look of loss. Her eyes were downcast and the veil of sorrow seemed to shadow her features over the normally radiant skin.

"Good morning, dear sister." James pulled out a chair for her. "Shall I serve you this morning?"

"Thank you. I can take care of myself in a moment. I appreciate your kindness."

"What can we do to bring joy back into your life?" Clare sat across from Grace.

"I wish I knew. I loved Braedyn. His life was snuffed out without reason and at such a young age." Grace leaned on her elbows with laced fingers and perched her chin on her hands. She gazed above Clare as if looking for her lost lover somewhere in the distance.

"I know you miss him terribly. Perhaps we can do something to cheer you up."

"What do you propose?"

"Shall we plan on a game night? We can have Father, Elizabeth, James, you and I play charades or cards. It'll make the time pass. These days can be dreary."

Grace exhaled. "I suppose it's better than sitting in my room feeling sorry for myself."

"It's settled." Clare smiled in hopes of cheering James's sister, well aware a game of cards would do nothing to cast the gloom aside. It seemed everyone was unhappy. Patrick. James and Grace. Father with issues surrounding Bethel Manor. And herself? She mustn't let the others pull her down. What good would it do if everyone lived under this pall of despondency?

Grace rose, filled a plate, returned to her chair and stared at the rising steam. James sat beside her and considered his food as if it were strange cuisine.

"Please. Can we just enjoy our meal with pleasure and not like we're attending a funeral?" Clare draped her serviette across her lap. "We've much to be thankful for. We're together as a family and have a warm home. Generous portions of food before us, good health, and God's goodness in many other ways."

James shrugged. "If we remain thankful, the rest falls into place."

"Exactly." Clare pierced a piece of meat with her fork.

The inner door slammed against the wall.

Abigail hastened in and curtsied. "Miss, I'm afraid there's a fight going on downstairs between two of the men."

James pushed his chair back and rushed after her. "We'll see about this."

"What do you suppose that's about?" Grace watched James bolt out the door.

Clare put her fork down. "I'm not certain, but it can't be good."

"That takes care of a relaxing morning, being thankful and trying to cheer ourselves."

"Seems everything's going against this becoming a blessed new year." Clare pushed her plate aside. "What in the world is happening to our happy home?"

Chapter Eight

James dashed into the main kitchen where boiling pots jiggled on the stove and food remnants on half-empty platters were dispersed along the large pine table. Flour was scattered over the floor and two lads scuffled like animals caught in a cage. "Stop it right this minute!"

Both lads were young. If either were thirteen years of age, James would be surprised. Being new staff, he had yet to learn their names.

He grabbed each by their collar and pulled them apart. "What's going on here?"

"He nicked the food I was savin'." The smaller of the two, brown hair shooting like fork tines from every angle of his scalp, reached around James as if to throttle the other with his fists.

"Did no such thing." The other lad, more muscular with half his right ear missing, jumped around like a jackal under James's hold.

"Saw you sneaking around and putting somethin' in your pocket."

"Why would he steal from anyone?" James nodded at the fare-covered table. "There's plenty to go around."

"He's a thief, that's why." The young scrapper continued to grapple against James's clutch.

"Stop struggling. We can talk this out like adults. What's your name?"

"Finley." The lad stopped floundering and wiped the back of his trousers with a swift movement of his hand.

"And yours?"

"Lucas, sir."

"Well, Finley and Lucas, it seems there's been a misunderstanding. Let's take this to the other room. Away from the rest of the staff." James directed an order to a maid. "Go find Sam and ask him to come, please."

What would they ever do without Sam and Jean, who oversaw much of the day-to-day running of the lower living quarters? Where was Jean, the stabilizing force for the home? She was usually front and center of the massive table, constantly making breads, pastries and soups.

James closed the door to the small office and directed the lads to sit. "We will get this sorted and you'll go back to work. Understand?"

Lucas growled at Finley, leaned forward on his chair and pointed. "So long's he don't say

I's a thief again. Else he might end up—"

"End up where." Finley shot up. "You makin' threats?"

"Sit down!" James planted himself between the chairs and pushed them back into their seats. "No bullying or fighting will be tolerated. Do I make myself clear?"

They nodded, both wearing scowls like children being reprimanded by a parent.

Sam entered, his coat covered with white powder that melted in minutes of entering the warm room. His normally toothless grin formed into a thin line. "What are these lads up to now?"

"They've fought before?" James asked.

"Whenever our backs are turned. Like siblings who never get along."

"This needs to stop or you'll have to be relieved from duty." James directed controlled anger towards Finley and Lucas.

Sam brushed wet droplets of melted snow from his clothing. "I'd behave if I were you. Believe me, you blokes don't want to be put out in this. Matter of fact, to keep you from getting into another scuffle, get a heavier coat and come with me. There are plenty of duties out in the cold for the two of you. It'll show how's you don't want to end up without a place to live."

The lads bowed their heads. "Do we have to?"

Finley's spiked hair seemed to flatten

somewhat with his downcast look. "It's bitter."

Sam pulled him up by his collar. "Go find a coat, and don't make me have to tell you again."

As the two left, James turned to Sam. "Thanks. Is Jean well? I haven't seen her in the house the past few days?"

"Seems she's troubled with a womanly problem. She'll be back in no time."

"Are you certain there's nothing we can do?" He touched Sam's shoulder.

"Thank you for asking, Master Blackwell. My Jean will be back to her kitchen soon. The household can't run without her."

The concerned look on Sam's face did not reassure James. "If there's anything you need for her let us know. In the meantime, we'll have one of the other girls step up and take over her duties."

"Thank you, sir. It'll put Jean's mind to rest. She's as mean as a hornet when she can't be cooking, I tell ya." Sam snickered slightly as if to relieve unspoken fears.

"We'll check on her tomorrow, if it's acceptable? I'm sure Clare misses her as much as the rest of us. If not more." He squeezed the old man's shoulder and departed.

+ + +

James made his way up the stairs to the main living area where Elizabeth and Clare both held sewing projects. "Did either of you know

Jean was ill?"

"I had no idea." Elizabeth opened a sewing chest and placed her work inside.

. "Nor did I." Clare ceased stitching. "I must see to her immediately."

"Sam seems to think she'll be fine in a matter of days."

"We'll have Doctor Willard check on her," Elizabeth said.

James shook his head. "I don't believe he could make it in this weather. As soon as it clears some we'll go for him."

"In the meantime, we can visit Jean." Clare rose and put her work aside.

"I told Sam you'd check on her tomorrow, but I'm sure she'd appreciate seeing you both today."

Elizabeth and Clare exited and James sat in the quietness for a few minutes. Sam's fretful behavior about Jean was disturbing to say the least. And now fights among the staff. There seemed to be no end to disputes and unsettled issues. Surely they were due good news for a change. Something to bring cheer to the close quarters they found themselves in. No one was going anywhere anytime soon and trying to bring some pleasure to an unpleasant time seemed impossible.

James slapped the settee and rose. There was no reason they couldn't make the best of the situation and find something productive to keep them occupied for the time being.

Chapter Nine

Clare scrunched her hands further into the muff as wispy, breath-formed clouds swirled around her mouth and eyes. Open blue skies, bright sunshine, albeit icy air, fashioned a wonderland of sparkling beauty. Echoes of the crunching snow under their feet swept across the field. "The surface glitters like jewels."

"Each season has its distinct beauty. They demonstrate God's creative variety, don't you agree?" Elizabeth bent, ladled a handful of snow and patted the lump into a perfect ball. She tossed it at Clare's feet and giggled like a toddler.

"It's like that, is it?" She laughed, pulled out a hand from the muff, picked up the small wad, threw it in Elizabeth's direction and ran ahead.

Elizabeth sprinted and caught up. "Isn't it marvelous?"

"The snow?"

"Being childish. Reliving how to play again. We quickly forget these things as we age."

"When George gets older we'll show him how it's done, shall we?" Clare slid her left hand into the crook of Elizabeth's arm and carried the muff with the other. This woman, James's mother, had brought such joy to Clare's father and herself.

Elizabeth had also walked with Clare through the hardest days of her life. She'd spoken truths, given her books in Braille, and taught her how to sew. Clare loved Elizabeth far more than she would ever realize.

They strolled down the lane several meters from the pillared entrance of Bethel Manor and headed to Sam and Jean's cottage nestled in a small treed area near the stables where Sam spent a good portion of his time.

Clare halted and removed her hand from Elizabeth's arm. "How strange."

"What is?"

"I've never come to this home when there hasn't been smoke coming from the kitchen chimney. Or lit candles displayed in the front windows, even on a bright day." She stepped up to the door and knocked. It was a tiny place, knitted into a warm and inviting home over the fifty years since Sam and Jean had begun to work at Bethel. Father had been a mere infant.

She knocked again.

"Do you suppose we should go in?" Elizabeth whispered as if afraid to wake the dead.

Clare opened the door and stepped inside. "Jean?"

Loud coughs came from upstairs.

They made their way up the narrow stairs in the center of the compact entranceway and turned right. "Jean?"

Curtains were drawn, and the odor of illness permeated the bedroom. One lone candle, burned down to a nub, flickered on a side table.

"Oh, my dear friend." Clare knelt beside the bed and grabbed Jean's hand. "How long have you been suffering?"

Jean turned and moaned with the slight movement. "Not long, miss. I'm sure I'll be fine in no time."

"We must get the doctor here," Elizabeth said.

"There's no need for him to come." Jean struggled in an attempt to sit.

"Be still. We'll get word to Father. I'm sure he'll want you seen and do whatever it takes to bring Doctor Willard here. In the meantime, I won't leave you."

"Thank you, miss."

Elizabeth's strained facial features confirmed Clare's own distress. "Please go and tell Father."

Elizabeth left and the candle flickered as

if to follow in her stead.

"When Sam was hurt last year, I thought my life had ended," Jean mumbled in low tones.

"Shhh. You must rest."

"Should anything happen to me he wouldn't know how to tie his shoes, never mind his tie for church." Jean choked on another cough.

"You must be quiet. There'll be no talk of you going anywhere. We...I need you." She swallowed hard.

Jean patted the top of Clare's hand with the same gentle touch she'd used many times. Those years when Clare's mother had died. When she often misunderstood her father, Jean had given her comfort with these same hands.

What would Sam do without her? What would their home *be* without this precious woman? Clare slipped out of the room to regain her composure. Even though outside the landscape sparkled, inside the dim walls darkness reigned.

+ + +

"I'm not sure how much more we can handle." Fredrick folded his hands over a letter sitting on his desk. "I've recently received word from Patrick Tripp he intends to take us to court."

"For what?" James sat upright on the seat opposite Fredrick.

"He's claiming you overstepped your

bounds in entering Willow Field without his knowledge. He's also stating there are family heirlooms missing."

"How ludicrous." James jumped up, circled the chair, and gripped its back.

"I agree. According to this letter, however," he tapped the envelope, "he's quite serious."

"Guess that's another good reason we didn't travel as first planned. We wouldn't have known this was his intent."

"I agree."

"Phoebe can't possibly be aware of this. She'd be aghast. I could go to her and—"

"You will go nowhere near Willow Field. Do I make myself clear?"

"What do you propose I do?"

"I suggest *you* do nothing. Let me speak with our lawyers and ask what our recourse might be."

James slapped the top of the chair. "And here I had come to ask about offering a sleigh ride with the horses or maybe clearing an area and having a bonfire. Something as a surprise for the others to replace the delayed trip."

"Those are wonderful suggestions. I'm afraid they must be postponed. For the time being." Fredrick joined James. "We'll resolve this issue somehow. I'm sure Patrick is striking out due to his pain. Maybe I should go and see him myself. Offer another type of recompense."

"How can you offer anything to clear my name? To imply I took something is beyond reasoning." James exhaled. "I'm sorry for putting everyone through this. What stupidity on my part."

Rap. Rap.

"Come in," Fredrick said.

"Hurry. You must do something." Elizabeth panted, her face pulsating with red splotches.

"My dear, what is it? You look awful. Come. Sit." Fredrick guided her to James's chair.

"There's no time. You must send for the doctor. Quickly. It's Jean." She burst into tears.

"What's happened?"

"She's terribly ill. I'm afraid…she's dying."

Chapter Ten

"There's no time to waste." Fredrick and James scrambled from the office. Elizabeth followed close behind.

Fredrick said, "James, Sam should be at the stables. Get him home. Have one of the other stable hands prepare two horses, Freya being one. I'll personally ride out and get Doctor Willard."

"Yes, sir." James gathered his boots and heavy cloak and departed.

"Elizabeth, please go and stay with Clare and Jean until I return. Sam needs the two of you for moral support."

"Be careful." Tears continued to course down his wife's cheeks, but the firmness in her eyes told him she had regained internal composure.

"I will. I promise." Fredrick hugged her quickly and ran through to the kitchen.

"Abigail, get two wool blankets and as many towels as you can gather. Get the towels over to Sam's cottage."

The girl remained in the center of the room and merely cocked her head.

"Did you hear me, girl?" Fredrick held his anger in check.

Clare's personal maid turned with a huff and stomped away to the other side of the table.

"Where are you going? I asked you to retrieve blankets and towels."

"I'm sorry, sir. I'm busy." Abigail picked up a rolling pin and proceeded to press a crust firmly into a perfectly concentric circle.

"You're what? You insubordinate child, I'll take care of you upon my return." He rushed into the linen closet, climbed a small stepladder and reached for the items he'd requested.

Fredrick stared angrily at Abigail as he walked past the table and pointed in her direction. "Be assured, your behavior won't be forgotten. And when you're finished with what you are doing, take these towels to Sam's cottage for the doctor's arrival." He laid the stack on another counter cleared of any food.

She pushed harder on the crust.

With emergency items bundled together, two blankets, his winter attire and boots, he headed to the backdoor.

The vacancy left by Jean was magnified by the young maid's insubordination. Times were changing, and he would give anything to bring Jean back here to her proper place. She would know well and good how to take care of this girl.

He slammed the door on his exit.

Freya was aging as surely as he was, but Fredrick trusted none of the other horses to carry him through this weather. They owned faster steeds, but she was sure-footed and reliable. He grabbed the reins from the stableman and swung his legs over Freya's inky, smooth hide and settled into the saddle.

"Here's the other animal you requested, sir." The stable hand offered him another set of reins to a horse needed for the doctor.

"Thank you." At least one staff member knew his job and did what he was told.

The young man touched his cap's bill and stepped away. "Take care, sir."

"I will." He clucked his tongue and drew his heels into the horse's middle. "Okay, girl, give everything you have. We're in a hurry."

Freya bolted and they traveled through the fields, out the pillared entrance and down the country road. The horse seemed to instinctually understand how dire the situation truly was.

+ + +

Clare paced the short hallway. Two other small rooms jutted from the passageway. She peered into the semi-darkness of the room closest to where Jean rested. Doilies draped an oversize chair and a small cot sat under the window. The difference in Clare's sizable bedroom compared to this meager accommodation was not lost on her. She sat in the chair, closed her eyes and folded her hands. "Father, God, You are the healer of mankind. Please restore my dear friend. Should You choose to take her home to You, I would be most jealous..."

Forceful beat of footsteps reverberated up the stairway and down the hall. Clare peered out as Sam and Elizabeth entered Jean's room.

Clare joined the others. "She's been resting peacefully. I stepped out for a minute to pray."

Sam pulled up a chair and took hold of his wife's hand and rubbed the fragile skin with miniature strokes. "Come on, girl. Wake up. I need you."

Elizabeth waited at the foot of the bed. "Her breathing's very shallow."

"She'll be fine. She's had her troubles before." Sam scooted closer to the bed and caressed Jean's forehead.

"Fredrick has gone for the doctor," Elizabeth said.

"My lady will be upset we've put the doctor out and caused them to ride in this weather." He brushed damp hair away from Jean's temples.

"Father doesn't mind. Jean means the world to him." She caught a choke in her throat.

"She'll recover. Won't she, Miss Clare?" Sam asked despairingly, his frightened tone shook.

"I'm not sure, Sam. We'll have to wait and see what Doctor Willard says."

"He healed you. I'm sure he'll take care of her." Sam gazed at Jean.

For a brief moment, the two seemed transported in time and Clare saw them as young lovers. Their deep wrinkles faded from view and the softened profiles were like silhouettes on an artist canvas. Love lasting a lifetime. She and James would one day face each other to say goodbye like this, and her heart yearned for the same unfathomable intimacy.

Jean seemed to sense Sam's presence, her tone raspy, "What ya doing? Why're you not with the animals?"

"Master James is with them. Told me to come home. Besides, I need to be with you."

She smiled weakly. "You silly man. Don't you know, I'm always with you? No matter where, I'm by your side." Jean coughed and Sam scooped his hand behind her back and raised her slightly.

"You know I love you," Sam whispered.

Jean looked at Elizabeth and Clare and coughed again. "Ladies, you take care of him for me. He'll need you."

Clare nodded and their blurred shapes seemed to float underwater. "You know we will."

Sam gently released Jean and her breathing seemed to draw less and less until it finally stopped altogether.

Sam rose from the chair, lay prone over his beloved's body and wept.

Chapter Eleven

Doctor Willard's office wasn't far, but considering the conditions along the lane, Fredrick watched every step and kept his pace to a reasonable trot. Although Freya was competent, the other animal's hesitancy made the circumstances more hazardous. With one misstep or jumpy reaction from the horse, they could easily tumble down an incline. He had no intention of letting that happen. He must get the doctor back to Bethel Manor.

Had Elizabeth overreacted about Jean's ailment? He hadn't stopped to think this trek might not be necessary. His wife was no fool and wouldn't send him out on an errand of this magnitude unless she knew it was unavoidable. No, Jean was obviously in grave danger.

Jean. Her rotund face and huge smile appeared before his mind's eye. She overflowed with an abundance of love. Her contagious laughter and long-suffering behavior was a testimony to everyone who knew her, especially him.

"Why, Master Fredrick, why are you thinking twice about marrying Miss Elizabeth?" Jean had gently reprimanded him when he had doubted the possibility.

"She might not love me. I'm older than her. She's beautiful."

His rationalizing hadn't fazed Jean. "*Tsk, tsk.* You claim to trust God with your life. You're afraid, why don't you admit it?"

They had laughed at her ability to pinpoint the exact reason he hesitated. It wasn't long afterward Elizabeth had agreed to marry him.

Jean had been his nanny as a child. Over the years, as he had matured, taken over the responsibilities of Bethel Manor and lost his parents, she became a dear friend. When his Florence had died she was his rock. What would life be like without her? Perish the thought. She needed to be seen by Doctor Willard. He would care for her and everything would return to normal. Yet a sense of dread seemed to take his thoughts captive.

He leaned nearer Freya's neck. For her protective warmth, and for the comfort and assurance everything would turn out fine.

Doctor Willard's office was in an adjacent wing to his moderate-sized estate. The building's brick exterior was plain except for a thick, twisted wisteria root traveling up the edge of the house's left side. In spring, its draped empty branches high above the main entrance would provide a striking drape of lavender colored blooms.

The office door opened and a beam of light spread across the gravel. Doctor Willard emerged, his form haloed in the doorway. "My dear man, what are you doing out on a day like this? Come in, before you catch your death from cold."

Fredrick hopped down from the horse. "There's no time to waste. Can you come with me to see after Jean?"

"Let me inform my wife. Otherwise Tess will begin to worry when I don't appear for dinner."

Doctor Willard disappeared for a moment and returned carrying an overcoat, hat, and satchel. "Are you positive you don't want to come in and warm up a few minutes before heading back home?"

"I'd rather not, but thank you for the offer. "I've brought along a blanket to wrap around yourself as the wind is quite sharp."

The doctor placed the latest headgear known as a bowler hat on his thinning hair. He mounted the horse, settled his bag and blanket in place, and they headed back to the manor.

No words were shared as they focused on

the terrain.

Approaching the pillared entrance to Bethel Manor, Fredrick stopped. He took a deep breath and allowed the doctor to ride ahead. "Lord, help me accept Your will."

Slowly, he followed. Time was of the essence, but he also knew he had to prepare for the worst. His family would count on him to step up and be like the pillars they had just passed through and served as a reminder to their guests they were in a place of safety. Fredrick would be expected to offer strength regardless of how they found Jean. If she were seriously ill, it would take time and a great deal of care to bring her back to full health.

Doctor Willard was already in the front door of the cottage when Fredrick arrived. The door was slightly ajar and he could hear the low buzz of voices and others crying.

"How is she?" Fredrick entered the foyer.

The murmuring stopped, and the red-rimmed eyes of Elizabeth and Clare focused on him. Neither said a word.

Sam stopped midway in the stairwell. The doctor was at the top of the stairs, disappeared around the corner and presumably into Jean's bedroom.

The world seemed to move in slow motion and Fredrick's legs became heavy as if they were planted in thick fen mud.

Before he knew it, Clare and Elizabeth

had their arms draped around him. His daughter wept as she did when she was a child.

A pillar. He needed to find the strength to hold his family together, conjure up the right words to comfort them and express faith in a loving, heavenly Father. Instead, he held his daughter and wife and wept as Sam walked slowly down the stairs and outside.

Fredrick released the two women, went outside and stepped up next to Sam. "Come inside, please."

"What'll I do without her?" Sam mumbled.

"You'll grieve. And never forget her. As I've done with Florence. No one will forget Jean. Although she's gone, her presence is everywhere." Fredrick placed an arm around his friend's shoulder.

Sam released a quiet groan. "Think I'll go to the horses now, sir, if you don't mind."

Fredrick removed his arm. "Do what you must. Work is a man's gift from God to give purpose when he doesn't know what else to do."

Sam labored slowly down the path. His world was forever changed and Fredrick knew only too well how the loss would become a gaping hole in Sam's heart.

With heaviness of spirit, Fredrick went back inside the cottage

Doctor Willard came down the stairs. "I'm sorry I didn't get here sooner, but I'm not sure there would've been anything I could have done. After Sam described her symptoms, it seems pneumonia had penetrated her lungs. Along with her age, it was impossible for her to fight back."

Fredrick hung his head.

Doctor Willard clasped Fredrick's forearm and squeezed. "I had a colleague tell me when a loved one dies, we get the privilege to watch them go from this life to a greater, more beautiful place they'll enjoy forever. Jean is truly home now."

Fredrick had hoped he would have been the one with words to inspire. Yet this family doctor had offered hope when all seemed lost. "I needed to hear your wisdom. Our home was made grander by her life while she was here, but Jean is indeed in a more wonderful place and will make it grander with her presence."

Chapter Twelve

Fredrick sat at his desk. A stack of white linen cards, trimmed with a thin, black border, beckoned to be written and addressed. Individual notes needed to be sent to friends announcing the passing of Jean. Although she had been an employee, he had never considered her as such. And those who knew him well knew she was as dear to him as any member of his family.

He pulled out the hunter-case pocket watch from his vest and flicked the latch open. Another thirty minutes had passed since he last checked. How could the rhythm of life keep its course when he wanted time to go in reverse? He wished he had taken the time to check in on Jean when he knew she had been unwell. At least he could have said farewell. He closed the watchcase and placed it back in the vest pocket. The tempo of time marched on.

Doctor Willard had returned home to organize details for Jean's body to be prepared while he, the ladies and James had returned to Bethel Manor. This place had always been a sanctuary from the pall of death.

Fredrick dug into the deep recess of his desk drawer and retrieved his clay pipe and tobacco.

"I haven't seen you use a pipe since just before our wedding." Elizabeth, now donned in elegant black attire had poked her head around the corner.

He placed the pipe back in the drawer. "I suppose it's my comfort when I don't know what else to do."

Elizabeth sat delicately on the chair across from him. Even in mourning clothes she was beautiful.

"It's been a shock to everyone. Poor Sam doesn't know what to do with himself. One minute he's in the stables, the next he's in the kitchen as if looking for Jean."

"Sadly, we need to hire someone to take her place."

"Must you think about it at this time?" Elizabeth's brow furrowed and concern carved thin lines alongside her mouth.

"It's difficult. But her duties must be attended to."

"May I be of assistance?"

Fredrick sighed. "Perhaps, but I was

thinking of asking Clare. Would you mind terribly if I asked her instead? It will keep her busy."

"Of course not. But isn't there someone we already employ who could handle her tasks? Perhaps Abigail?"

"I'm afraid we must dismiss Abigail." Her disrespectful attitude caused Fredrick's inner grief to transfigure into irritation. He clenched his fingers into fists.

"Clare's maid?"

"She refused to obey when I asked her to help with gathering blankets and towels. Her unruly behavior could be a bad influence on the others."

"Would you like me to speak with her? It seems cruel to discharge her directly after Jean's passing." Elizabeth dabbed her eyes with an embroidered handkerchief.

"If you wish. Or have Clare attend to it since she's her maid. If the girl continues with disruptive actions, she'll be given notice. Please pass this on to Clare."

"Mister Shaw?" Everett, a staff member who had proven worthy enough to become his manservant bowed at the waist as he waited in the entrance to the office.

"Yes, what is it?"

"Two men have arrived who wish to speak with you. Shall I ask them to come back at a more convenient time?"

"Two men? I hope this isn't about the infernal legal document I received from Patrick Tripp. If it is, I'm not sure I can deal with them as a true gentleman ought to." He rose, shoved his chair back and dismissed the servant. "Never mind, Everett, I'll see to them myself."

"Are you sure you should?" Elizabeth stood and held his arm with a sympathetic touch as he walked by her.

He patted her hand. "I'll be fine. Thank you."

Fredrick tugged on his vest and entered the foyer. "Now see here, gentlemen…"

A looming figure turned, rushed at him and swept Fredrick into a tight hug.

"Thomas?" Fredrick stepped back. "What in the world are you doing here?"

James had met Thomas and Braedyn in Ely when he had first arrived in East Anglia looking for his family. It wasn't long before the two men had become part of Bethel Manor and dear friends of Fredrick.

"Heard about Miss Jean. Came as fast as I could."

"I know news gets passed along quickly, but how did you learn about this in Ely?"

"When a staff member starts to share in one household, the entire world learns faster than it takes for a streak of lightening to pass over the sky."

"I'm grateful you've come."

A man stepped from the shadows.

"Braedyn?" Fredrick nearly collapsed. Thomas reached out and held his elbow.

This man had the same fiery red, bushy hair and familiar mustache Braedyn had worn.

"But it's...not possible," Fredrick said.

"Meet Braedyn's brother, Michael."

"The similarity is uncanny." Fredrick held out a hand and the men shook.

"Pleasure to meet you, sir." Michael smiled.

"The pleasure is mine. Your brother was a man of courage and I admired him greatly. He went on a journey with me to Bristol and helped carry supplies to an orphanage when it wasn't required of him."

"I heard about your trek from Thomas. Plus, Braedyn had written home about you and your family."

Thomas rubbed his hands together as if to warm them.

"How uninviting I've been. You must excuse me. Please come in to the sitting room and thaw yourselves. I'll have warm drinks brought in straight away," Fredrick pulled the cord for the servants, who entered and received the order for tea.

The men moved to where the blaze gave off a snug atmosphere and stopped in front of the fireplace with their hands outstretched.

"Let me go and bring the others. I know

they'll experience great delight seeing you both. We could use a little joy right now."

Fredrick paused. "I have missed your brother tremendously, Michael."

"As have I. But I am grateful for your friendship towards him."

"I hope we can soon become friends as well."

"As do I."

Fredrick left as the tea was brought in. The sensation Braedyn had somehow come back into their life in a small way gave him hope Jean would never be far away either. There were too many memories of her for him to ever forget.

Grace came down the stairs dressed in black, Parramatta silk. "Father, did I hear voices?"

"Yes, my dear, and I'm certain you'll enjoy meeting one of our two guests."

He escorted her into the sitting room.

When Grace saw Michael on the settee, she fainted in Fredrick's arms.

Chapter Thirteen

"Are you feeling better, my dear?" Fredrick held a small flask of smelling salts under Grace's nose. They had managed to move her onto the settee and prop her feet on a pillow.

She shifted her head back and forth, wrinkling her nose at the pungent odor. "I thought I saw...an apparition." Grace propped herself up slightly. "I'll be fine. For a brief moment, I was convinced Braedyn was here among us."

Michael came around from the back of the settee. "Please don't faint again, Miss. Brae was my brother, and I'm no ghost." He smiled and bowed his head.

"Oh, my." Grace waved a petite fan in front of her face. "I wasn't imagining him after all."

"What's the fuss going on? We heard noise when we were heading to the kitchen."

James entered, followed by Elizabeth. His eyes widened as his gaze fell on one of the visitors. "Thomas?"

The two men seized each other by the arms. Friendship brothers. Fredrick knew how much James admired this strapping man who had brought James to meet his long-lost family. Their reunion had been bittersweet. Bitter because James's father had already passed away, sweet because he was united with his sister, Grace, and his mother. There was much jubilation when the two women relocated to Bethel Manor and Elizabeth became Fredrick's wife.

"It's been too long." Thomas held James at arm's length. "Seems the fare is mighty good here. Looks like you've filled out some." He chuckled deep and long.

Elizabeth hugged Thomas. "What a sweet surprise."

"And you, milady, have grown lovelier with each passing year." He grew somber. "I'm only sorry we've come at the expense of your grief. Jean was a fine lady if there ever was one."

"She was indeed," Fredrick said. "But we are being neglectful not introducing Braedyn's brother, Michael."

"It's as if Braedyn were back with us." Elizabeth curtsied slightly. "What an honor to meet you."

Michael's red Irish coloring deepened and

his thick mustache twitched.

"Ah, I see you have the same display of embarrassment as your brother." Fredrick clapped Michael's back and released a chuckle. How wonderful to find a source of happiness when pain was merely inches deep.

"Where's Clare? Michael must meet the tiniest yet most determined creature to have ever lived." Thomas teased.

"Jean used to call her a force of nature. She's calmed down under James's watchful eye," Fredrick said.

"Let me retrieve her." James left and chatter ensued.

Michael drew closer to Grace and grew serious. "I'm sorry I startled you. Are you feeling better?"

Grace lowered her eyes. "Yes, thank you."

"She loved Braedyn." Fredrick stepped up to them.

"And he cared for Grace very much. He spoke about her oft to the family." Michael's eyes clouded when he mentioned home.

"How are they? Braedyn always had such concern for them."

"The Eire famine seems to be improving, but severe tensions have arisen. This fiasco has become a rallying point for movements everywhere. People are fed up with the disgraceful conditions thousands have gone through without recourse."

"These are frightful times. Many were dispersed because of the blight, and uprisings are occurring wherever there are enough men to cause a ruckus," Fredrick said.

"Let's change the subject, shall we?" Elizabeth took his arm. "We're here to remember our dear friend, Jean, and rejoice in this reunion. Let's not spoil it."

"You're right, my dearest."

"Tell us more about yourself, Michael." Grace placed her feet on the floor, collapsed the fan and glanced up at him. "Are you older or younger than Braedyn?"

"I'm a wee bit younger but everyone always thought I was the oldest as I was forever savin' Brae from troubles."

"What kind of troubles?" Grace prodded, a slight smile curling along her mouth.

Fredrick took Elizabeth by the elbow and directed her to the other side of the room, whispering along the way, "Shall we give them time to get to know one another?"

"Why, Fredrick, surely you aren't playing matchmaker?" Her eyes twinkled, and the creased lines of concern from earlier softened into thin crinkles of delight.

"What would ever give you such an idea?"

Clare burst into the room. "Is it true? Thomas, dear, dear man. You are *here*."

"Mistress Clare." He bent and touched

the top of her hand with his lips.

"It's wonderful to see you." Clare diverted her direction around Thomas's broad shoulders. "You must be Braedyn's brother."

Michael bowed. "Yes, ma'am."

"Now that we have everyone together we consider family, shall we say a prayer of thanks?" Fredrick could hardly contain his emotions. The mixture of joy and sorrow mingled as they closed their eyes, folded hands and he prayed for his friends who had passed and thanked God for the joy of meeting someone new.

+ + +

"Must you go? It seems as if you've only just arrived." Clare and the others escorted Thomas and Michael to the front entranceway.

Everett held the men's cloaks in preparation for their departure.

"We must get back to Ely. My wife and wee ones are going to be wondering where I've been. But we'll be back." Thomas nodded at Michael who lingered with Grace in an alcove. "I'm certain of it."

"How wonderful to see my sister's countenance brighten," James said.

"It is indeed." Clare smiled.

Everett helped the men slide on their cloaks and offered them their caps. The manservant opened the door and a gust of wintertime swept in.

"Take care everyone." Thomas prepared to leave as someone approached the alcove entrance. "Why, Miss Phoebe what are you doing out in this weather?"

Thomas stepped aside and Phoebe entered with her two children. "I've come for a place of refuge. I do believe my Patrick has gone completely mad."

Chapter Fourteen

"Come in out of this drafty foyer and warm yourself. It's dreadfully cold outside." Fredrick held out an arm for each of Phoebe's children. "Everett, ring for the nursery maid and let's get these babies settled with George Andrew. There's plenty of space for them to sleep there."

The butler departed to summon the maid.

"How old are you now, Sara?" Fredrick bounced the girl lightly and she held up three pudgy fingers.

"And Daniel Joseph, your younger brother, is only a baby, isn't he?" He held the infant close to his chest with his other arm.

Sara put fingers over her mouth and giggled. "He doesn't know how to wawk yet."

"Ah, but you're a clever girl. You already know how to *walk*, don't you?"

She nodded. The golden curls beneath her

winter hat jiggled, and her wide eyes, similar to her mother's, resembled miniature blue globes.

Fredrick handed the infant to the maid who had hurried into the foyer. He placed Sara on the floor and the child took hold of the servant's hand.

"Thank you." Phoebe trembled as her coat swayed slightly. "I knew I could rely on this family even with Patrick's unfavorable conduct."

"What a travesty. He has no reason to be this judgmental." James stepped up, arms opened, as if to hug her.

Phoebe retreated a step. "I keep trying to speak sense into him, but he won't listen. He's threatening to take everything away from you, including this estate. How he thinks he'll manage is beyond me."

Fredrick came between Phoebe and James and faced her. "I'd planned to go and visit him. See if we can't sort through this mess together."

"I'm not sure that's a good idea. He's acting very foolishly. Who knows though, maybe he'll listen to you." Phoebe flushed face resulted from being outside and the obvious anger against her husband.

"How in the world did you manage to get here?" Elizabeth took Phoebe's hand and led her to the sitting room.

"Patrick had the carriage prepared to go visit his solicitor, but then changed his mind for some unknown reason. I decided to use it myself. I've sent the driver back home. I hope I'm not being too presumptuous in coming?"

"You are not. You're welcome to stay as long as necessary."

"He's so unlike himself. I know he wouldn't hurt the children, but his anger is uncontrollable at times. He paces like a wild animal."

Thomas drew his cloak tighter. "I'm sorry, but we must be off. Michael and I will return in a few days."

"Thank you again for your visit. We look forward to seeing you soon," Fredrick said.

Michael gave one last glance in Grace's direction, smiled broadly and the two men left.

"What a striking resemblance to Braedyn," Phoebe said.

"The similarity is truly remarkable. Now let's stop standing in the draft and go into the sitting room."

The activity in the house distracted Fredrick, and he wouldn't manage to get the announcements about Jean out at this rate if he didn't make a polite exit. "If you'll excuse me, I'm sure Elizabeth and Clare will take good care of you. James, please come with me into my office for a moment."

Phoebe released Elizabeth's hand and hugged Fredrick. "Thank you again. I do pray you are able to sort this out. But I'm not sure you'll be able to resolve my marriage. It seems it's beyond hope."

"Hush. We won't hear of it. Patrick will come around." James moved closer to Phoebe.

"James. My office, please," Fredrick said sharply as they left the sitting room.

"Yes, sir."

James tilted his head as Fredrick closed the office door behind them. "What can I do to offer my assistance?"

Fredrick walked behind his desk. Could this man be senseless? "Are you unaware of why I've asked you to join me?"

"Do you wish for me to accompany you to the Tripp home and confront Patrick?"

"Could it be you're blind?"

"What do you mean?

"Do you not see the necessity to keep your distance from Phoebe?"

James expanded his chest. "What are you saying? I've done nothing to warrant your reprimand."

"Let me say this as clearly as possible. You will not, under any condition, be alone with Phoebe in this house. And you mustn't approach her for affection as you tried a moment ago. In your supposed innocence you could give Phoebe, never mind Clare, the wrong impression."

"Supposed innocence? Are you questioning my integrity?"

"I'm doing no such thing and you know

it. You also know what I'm saying is true. When Patrick hears his wife is under our roof, believe me he'll stop at nothing to cause us harm if it's his intent. I don't want to give him any more ammunition than he already has. Do you understand?"

James sat, slumped forward and cradled his head. "I've been extremely thoughtless. I'm sorry."

"From now on use discernment. If I know my daughter, Clare is going to be watching how you and Phoebe interact. Please don't give her any excuse to wonder about your faithfulness in this matter."

"Do you really think Clare would question my love?" James ran his fingers through his hair and stood. "I would never do anything to hurt her again."

"Bear that in mind. Your every action is being monitored." Fredrick loathed having to be harsh but everything depended on perception with the staff, never mind Phoebe who was extremely vulnerable.

"I understand. May I go now?"

"Yes. And please let this conversation remain between us. There are others besides Patrick trying to undermine our home. Let's not give anyone any further reason to gossip."

James shuffled out and closed the door.

Fredrick sat behind his desk. The announcements demanded his attention like small flags waiting to be waved, but he turned and gazed out at the darkening sky. Patrick was like a cauldron inside, ready to bubble over and spill his abhorrence of James on everyone in the family.

How could Fredrick stop Patrick's raging storm? He spun back to the desk, pulled one of the papers towards him and began to write.

Chapter Fifteen

James wasn't sure whether to kick or hit something. Instead, he picked up and threw the nearest object, a small Chinese vase sitting on a half-moon table in the foyer. The blue object spun in the air, landed with a soft thump in the bowl on the center table and sent green boughs spiraling.

Elizabeth peered out from the sitting room. "What in the world?"

"Sorry. It was an accident." Now he had lied to cover his anger. How could Fredrick think he would repeat the same mistake with Phoebe? James wanted to speak to Phoebe and reassure her of his concern. Nothing more.

Elizabeth pulled the door closed behind her, knelt on the floor and began gathering boughs.

"Please, don't. I can get the staff to clear up," James said.

She sat back on her haunches. "I was never raised to have someone else do my work. This will only take a few minutes."

He got on down beside her. "At Alpheton Orphanage there was never anyone else to do the work except us orphans."

They gathered the boughs and placed them back in the bowl. James resituated the vase in its proper place, while Elizabeth put finishing touches on the last two pieces of greenery and clapped her hands. "There. Just the way they were."

"Thank you." He exhaled.

"Is there something you'd like to talk about?"

"No. But I appreciate you asking." What could his mother possibly understand about how he felt with what had happened with Phoebe? And Fredrick's insinuation was totally uncalled for.

"If you're certain." She pecked him on the cheek and retreated back to the sitting room.

James circled the foyer. The door to the sitting room opened once more.

Phoebe's frame was shadowed as she came out. "Elizabeth said you had a slight accident. Are you unharmed?"

"Yes. I'm fine." James reached out and held her arms. "But are you? I'm sorry Patrick has gotten this upset."

Phoebe shrugged slightly to release his

grip. "I'm not sure what will happen with me and the children. We may end up with my parents, but they're unaware of what's going on right now and I'd like to keep it that way."

"We never meant to harm anyone, did we?"

She gazed at him and whispered, "No, but we should've known better."

"*Ahem.*" Clare stood at the top of the stairs.

James and Phoebe both jumped and backed away from each other.

"I heard a sound…merely checking…" Phoebe stammered.

"I hit the bowl and the boughs fell." James reached for out for Clare's hand. She pulled it behind her back.

"How tragic." Sarcasm dripped from Clare's tone. "Excuse me. I just finished assisting with putting the children down, and I must check on something in the kitchen."

"Can I help?" he asked.

"No. Thank you. I'm sure you and Phoebe have plenty to catch up on." Clare whirled around and left.

"Oh, dear. We've done it again," Phoebe said.

"Fredrick warned me Clare would be watching."

"I should've never come." Phoebe looked away.

"Yes, you should've. But I'm being an idiot thinking we can maintain the friendship we've had in the past."

"Don't you see, that's no longer possible?" Phoebe turned back and studied him. "Ever. Do you understand? I don't want to hurt you, James, but we can never speak without others around us ever again."

Abigail walked passed with a tray of tea and biscuits, glancing sideways under her white cap with a slight sneer curling her lip.

"What are you looking at?" James demanded.

"Why nothing, sir." The servant headed towards the sitting room.

Phoebe opened the door for the maid and they both entered.

Left alone in the cold foyer, James slapped his thigh and marched to the kitchen.

"May I speak with you, please?" He asked Clare, who directed a servant working by the stove.

"I'm busy."

"I'll wait." He crossed his arms.

"This could take time."

"I'll sit." James pulled out a chair and plopped down with a thud.

"What is it? Can't it wait?"

"No. I'd like to talk with you now." He softened his tone. "Please."

She spoke to the cook, "Be sure to rotate

the roast and keep your eye on it. We don't want it to dry out."

"Yes, miss."

Clare motioned to James and they went into the linen closet. "What's so urgent? You appeared rather busy yourself with Phoebe a moment ago." She pouted, hands on hips.

"I wanted to sort this out straight away and not leave you with any misconceptions of what was going on."

"What *is* going on, James? I thought we had worked through this and you had gotten over Phoebe."

"There was never any 'getting over Phoebe.'" He took her into his arms and gazed into the dark depth of her eyes. "I love *you*."

Clare shimmied out of his grasp. "What were you two talking about?"

"If you must know, I wanted to tell her I was sorry Patrick was acting difficult. It can't be easy with two children and a husband who has lost his mind."

"It's time you stayed out of Patrick and Phoebe's business."

"Your father said the same thing," James murmured.

"He did?"

"Yes, and he said you'd be watching me with Phoebe and how we behaved together. As if I were a child needing supervision."

"You aren't a child. You're allowed to do

whatever you please. But there are consequences to choices you make."

James pulled Clare close. "I've never regretted we chose each other. There's no one else I want to be with, and no one I love but you."

Clare's body relaxed in his arms.

He kissed her. "There'll never be anyone but you. And I don't want you to ever forget it."

She stepped back an inch. "And I don't ever want you to forget I'm watching," Clare teased, drew near and kissed him.

Chapter Sixteen

Fredrick carried a candle along the dark hallway, his finger curled inside the holder's ring. The flame flickered with his frosty breath as he passed the Longcase clock standing sentry duty midway along the hall.

Tick-tock. Tick-tock.

Its weight-driven pendulum clicked back and forth and chimed on the quarter-hour. Fredrick checked to be sure the weights didn't need to be raised. The Timothy Mason face, with its Roman numerals and sleek hands kept perfect time. Family and staff used the precision piece to keep the house running on schedule.

So where were the servants responsible for stoking the fires in each room? Winter months demanded they be attended to in the early hours to warm the house before everyone rose.

He made his way down the hall, walked

up winding stairs and made his way to the male servant quarters. Everett should have roused the men and had the fires taken care of by now.

Fredrick knocked on the servant's door. "Everett?"

The door opened and the tall, rumpled-clothed man rubbed his eyes. "Sir?"

"What's going on, man? The fires need to be tended."

Everett blinked as if waking from a deep stupor. "Sir? It's just gone midnight. We usually don't start until two, but if you wish me to begin now — ?"

"The Longcase says it's nearly three."

"So sorry, sir. I'm not sure how it happened. I'll get to it right away."

"Thank you." Fredrick wound his way down the stairs and continued to his office. There was no going back to sleep now.

He placed the taper down on his desk, threw kindling in the fireplace, and used the poker to stir warmed embers from last night's fire. He blew into his hands and rubbed them together. Although the temperatures were warming slightly, it would be several months before heating the house could be forgotten.

Everett arrived in Fredrick's office in minutes, fully dressed in uniform, and standing at attention. "I can't understand, sir, but I assure you, it won't happen again."

"These things occur. But next time, be

sure you inspect the clock for the correct time before retiring."

"What's strange, sir, is that I did. When I went to my room, I double-checked. It was eleven o'clock and I knew I had three hours for sleep. But I've only slept one."

"How odd. Never mind, be assured you won't lose your job over this minor infraction." Fredrick smiled wearily. "You're too valuable to me. To us."

Everett bowed. "Very kind of you to say, sir. Shall we start in this room?"

"I've managed to begin a small one in here, go to the others and get them stoked."

The servant bowed once more and left.

Fredrick swiped a palm along his face. Stubble had formed along his chin. In addition to warming the house, there would be a need to heat a great deal of water. The children and women needed to wash, as did he and the other men of the household.

Was he losing touch? It seemed he couldn't get the servants to do what was required. Others arrived late. A couple of them neglected their duties entirely. It may be time to pass responsibility of running the house over to James. Maybe he *was* getting too old.

"What in the world?" Elizabeth's long flowing sleeping gown hugged her figure. A short shawl lay draped over her shoulders.

He jolted.

"Oh dear, I didn't mean to startle you, but what are you doing here in the wee hours of the morning?"

She held a candle shoulder high. Her stance brought to mind a picture of a Pre-Raphaelite Mallais exhibit at the Royal Academy he'd once had the privilege to view. Although there was much controversy over Mallais' art form, Fredrick found them to be refreshingly detailed. Exquisite like his wife.

He rubbed his face again. "I couldn't sleep."

"What's troubling you? Is it the passing of Jean?"

"I'm sure that's a large part of it."

"I know you miss her terribly. She was a source of strength for everyone in this home."

"It's almost as if another part of my history's gone."

"I'm sorry for your loss. But it seems something else is bothering you. And I've always known you to have such peace in your spirit."

Fredrick moaned. "Sam. He's distraught, and I'm not sure what to say to him."

"God will give you the right words." She placed the candle down and perched on the edge of his desk facing him.

"Plus having Phoebe and the children here."

"How does that worry you?" Elizabeth

pulled her shawl tighter.

"I've no concern over them being here. Our home is always opened to those in need. But there can be many misunderstandings along the way."

"Is Patrick a cause of anxiety?"

"Somewhat. I plan on visiting him later. We must discuss this as gentlemen and see if we can't come to an understanding. His wife and children belong at home with him."

"Of course they do. And Phoebe wants that as well."

Fredrick calculated his words. "Are you positive?"

"What can you mean?" She moved and sat on the chair across from him.

"I always want to believe the best in people. Give them the benefit of the doubt. Part of me wonders if she isn't here to see James."

"You can't be serious?"

"Surely the thought passed through your mind," he said.

"I suppose. But to what end?"

"She misses the companionship. James offered a friendship her husband has forgotten to give. And in his anger, he's making the situation worse."

"So you think she's using this as a ruse to be with James?"

Fredrick smacked the desktop. "I don't know. It seems I don't know much these days."

Elizabeth rose, walked around the desk and positioned herself in front of him. "I know one thing. These doubts are unlike the man of strength and character I love. Where do you suppose these uncertainties are coming from?"

"I don't know." He shrugged. "I feel incapable of dealing with the servants, the magnitude of this place, those needing care."

"You're perfectly adept at handling these things but sometimes a burden is too heavy even for a man to carry. Thank you for sharing your heart. I do hope it gives you solace, along with the fact I believe in you." Elizabeth pressed her fingertips to her lips and blew. She pulled her shawl tighter, picked up the taper and departed.

"If only I believed in myself though."

Chapter Seventeen

Fredrick awoke and lifted his head from crossed arms. Brilliant light streamed through the window. A swath of warmth caressed his cheek. How much time had passed?

Babies crying, shuffling of feet and muffled voices filled the hallway outside his office door. The taper had burned to the base of its holder.

He rubbed his eyes and stretched.

Had Elizabeth actually come to him in the night? Or had he dreamed of her visit? She had said she believed in him. If only he could agree.

Fatigue lingered. It was as if he'd never slept. For a few moments, dizziness made the room spin. He touched his forehead. No fever.

Rap. Rap.

"Yes?" Fredrick answered. "Come in."

The door opened, and Everett entered. "Sir, a Mister and Missus Coulters are here to see you."

Phoebe's parents. He leapt from the chair, straightened his clothing and flattened his hair into place. "Give me a moment. Please take them into the sitting room and ring for tea."

"Yes, sir."

Once Fredrick was satisfied he looked presentable, he joined the Coulters. "Welcome, dear friends. It's been ages since I've seen you. Mary, you look wonderful. You never change."

Phoebe had definitely gotten her delightful looks from her mother.

"And I never look as if I need to eat more." Daniel, Phoebe's father, patted his oversized belly and laughed.

What a joy to hear laughter in the house.

Fredrick shook the man's hand. "It's such a pleasure to see you, both."

Mary grew serious. "I'm sorry, we shouldn't enjoy joviality in light of your loss. We were sorry to hear about Jean."

"Thank you. She was a delight to those who knew her. But she wouldn't want us to be mournful. It wasn't like her to be solemn."

"We remember the twinkle in Jean's eyes. And she was always ready to offer delicious pastries." Daniel smiled.

"Food." Mary winked at Daniel as she held his arm. "I'm afraid that's all my husband thinks about."

"My dear, that's not true. I think about

riding, the hunt, and long naps." He chuckled again.

"Please, sit." Fredrick directed. "Tea should be served shortly."

Mary and Daniel shared the settee.

"Refreshments aren't necessary. We merely stopped by to offer our condolences after receiving your notice."

"How kind." Fredrick cleared his throat. "So you're…unaware? You aren't here to see…" He hesitated. Should he mention Phoebe?

"To see whom?" Mary's eyebrow rose.

"Um."

Rap. Rap.

Phoebe entered. "Excuse me. I wondered if I could ask…Mother? Father? What are you—?"

The Coulters stood in unison. Mary said, "What a surprise. What are *you* doing here?"

Phoebe looked from Fredrick to her parents and threw back her shoulders. "I'm…a guest."

Daniel drew near his daughter. "Why would you need to be a guest in this home?"

"Patrick and I are having some…difficulties. We need time apart."

Mary said, "Why would you come to Fredrick and not your own family? To us?"

"I didn't want you to worry. Or think less of Patrick. We'll sort this out. But it'll take time."

"What has to be sorted? A wife needs to

be with her husband."

"I know, Father. But there are times a family shouldn't be together if the situation warrants."

"Has he caused you harm?" Mary asked with apprehension.

"No, Mother. He's confused. Nothing more."

"I should leave you to discuss this." Fredrick began to depart.

"Please stay," Phoebe said. "You're well aware of what's going on."

"You must return home immediately." Daniel's normally cheerful voice held a hard tone.

"I can't." Phoebe stomped her foot.

"You can't or you won't?"

"There needs to be an understanding between Patrick and me before I return."

"Perhaps you should explain what has caused this dispute to occur." Fredrick softly urged Phoebe. The last thing he wanted was to become involved in a family discussion, but Phoebe had a right to be heard.

Daniel turned to him. "Why didn't you notify us that our daughter was under your roof?"

"We thought we were friends." Mary pleaded.

"We *are* friends."

"It doesn't appear as if you're acting in

our best interests."

"Please don't take this out on Fredrick. You're doing him an injustice. You should be grateful he willingly took me and the children into his home," Phoebe said.

Daniel puffed out his chest. "Explain what has caused this dishonor to your husband."

"When Clare was unwell last fall, James wanted George Andrew to spend time with other children. He came to the house quite regularly." Phoebe rushed on. "Apparently one of the staff reported to Patrick James and I were spending an inordinate amount of time alone while he traveled."

"Rumors begin like this." Mary squeezed Phoebe's hand.

"We never intended…" Her voice broke and she sobbed in her mother's arms.

"There. There." Mary patted her daughter's back. "I'm sure this can be sorted."

"I was going to visit Patrick shortly myself. To see if he'll listen to reason." Fredrick held the door handle in preparation to leave.

"I'll accompany you," Daniel insisted.

"I'd rather you wouldn't. Patrick has sent a letter through a solicitor with charges against James. I would like to address these concerns with Patrick personally and see if we can come to an agreement."

"Patrick has done this?" Daniel eye's

widened. "How ludicrous."

"That's what I've been trying to say. He's not himself, and I don't know how to make him see nothing happened between James and me."

"Although he has reason to be upset, collaborating with a solicitor seems a bit dramatic." Daniel glanced from Fredrick to his daughter. "Trust has been broken in this situation and needs to be rebuilt."

"I agree, Father." Phoebe hung her head.

"If you'd like to stay here with Phoebe while I go to Willow Field, you are most welcome. Either Patrick will listen to what I have to say or he won't. If I'm unable to speak rationally with him, I may call on you for support." Fredrick put out a hand. "Please forgive me, Daniel. I had no intention of keeping anything from you."

Daniel shook his hand. "We'll work through this matter together. It may be better if we stayed at Bethel Manor and don't confuse the children further."

"Then I can tell Patrick the whole family's here. What do you say Phoebe?"

"I'd rather not disrupt the children again if it's agreeable to everyone. And hopefully we won't have to impose on you too long."

"As you wish." Fredrick stepped into the hall and exhaled. If only Patrick would be as forgiving as Daniel. But he had no expectations the exchange with him would be quite as easy.

Chapter Eighteen

"There seems to be a bit of lint along this shoulder." Fredrick observed himself in the oval mirror, turning slightly one way then another.

Everett swiped the brush across the back of Fredrick's shoulders and along the sides of the short jacket. "Is that sufficient, sir?"

"Much better." Greying along Fredrick's hairline had stretched from behind his ears midway up his temples. Elizabeth said she found it attractive. To him, the grey was another reminder of aging, along with the fine lines beside his eyes. Both were proof he was no longer the young man he used to be.

His servant's reflection showed a full head of black hair without a single silver streak.

Everett placed the brush down and tugged on the back of Fredrick's jacket. "Finished, sir."

"Wonderful. Thank you." He wanted to

present the highest standard possible to Patrick. He didn't need to impress him, but when a man challenged another it was best to demonstrate confidence and composure. Neither of which he felt.

Fredrick had no idea what to expect from Phoebe's husband. He couldn't blame the man for his feelings, but a sense of clear-headedness was obviously needed.

He stepped away from the mirror, took his overcoat, top hat and gloves from Everett and strode to the front door where a carriage should be waiting to take him to Willow Field.

The gravel drive was empty. He trudged inside and pulled the long tapestry cord hanging inside the foyer.

Everett reappeared within a few minutes. "Is something wrong, sir?"

"Could you please have one of the men go to the stables and see where my coach is? It was scheduled to be here by now."

"Indeed, sir." Everett rushed away.

What was happening? There seemed to be no end of disruptions.

"I thought you'd be gone by now." James came into view, as he approached from the corridor into the foyer.

"The carriage has been delayed."

"Shall I go and see what's caused the holdup?"

"I've sent Everett."

Wheels crunched along the gravel. Fredrick said, "Seems it's arrived. I'll be off now. In the meantime, maybe you can find out if Sam could use help. I know he's finding work difficult. It could explain why my ride wasn't here."

"I'll be sure to check on him."

Fredrick climbed the two steps and tapped the inside of the coach's hood.

His coachman slapped the reins and the horses snorted. The conveyance lurched as Fredrick arranged a blanket across his lap and settled back on the buttoned cushions.

Memories flashed back to riding in the same carriage with Braedyn when they had taken supplies to Bristol. He'd never forget the fateful trip when Braedyn had lost his life.

Barren fields passed outside the small window. God's earth went through seasons of transitions. Each one held a beauty, yet there was always a yearning for the next one to makes its debut. "Come on, man. Pull yourself together." He tucked the blanket tighter across his middle.

The ride to the Tripp household seemed to take ages, although in reality it was merely thirty minutes.

Willow Field sat in a valley. When the coach reached the crest approaching the long drive to the estate, he tapped the hood. "Hold up."

The carriage stopped.

Fredrick bowed his head and folded his hands. "Lord, give me wisdom. May Patrick hear and receive my words as they are intended. To offer him friendship and reconciliation. Amen."

He tapped the hood once more. "Move on."

In five minutes, the carriage pulled up in front of the house.

Patrick opened the door and beckoned Fredrick to enter. "Come in out of the cold." Patrick's strong American accent was firm and there was no warm reception as he helped Fredrick out of his overcoat. "I must say, I'm surprised to see you. Let's retire to the lounge, shall we?"

"It's good to see you, Patrick," Fredrick said as they entered the homey sitting room.

"Why don't you get to the point of why you're here."

Fredrick held out his hand. "I'm here to offer friendship."

Patrick turned away and walked to the other side, hands clasped behind his back. He wheeled around and stopped. "Why should I accept your gesture? I'm sure you are well aware of what has happened under this roof." He pointed upwards. "Deceit. Duplicity. I'm afraid our families can no longer remain close."

"I'm well aware of your consternation,

but I'd hoped we could speak as men and work through this in a civilized manner."

Patrick hit the back of the settee. "Civilized? How dare you speak to me of being civil when your son-in-law was anything but civil in my home." His voice escalated and veins along his neck pulsed with anger.

"There's no need to shout. Please."

Patrick inhaled deeply and exhaled. "I'm sorry. I've no reason to take this out on you. And I hold you no grudges against the Shaws'."

"Yet you send a notice from a solicitor you intend to take me to court."

"For James. Not you."

"My family is my responsibility. Whichever member you hold a grudge against."

"You did a poor job of taking care of *your* responsibility. You should have kept James from visiting *my* wife."

"Is there another way we can handle this? Both James and Phoebe sincerely regret they didn't inform you. They weren't trying to hide anything."

"And you believe them?"

Fredrick paused.

"You don't believe it yourself, do you?"

"I don't think they considered how James coming with George to visit with the children would look to the staff. I grant you, they should have been open and honest with you. However, I think there's a better way to deal with this."

"What do you propose?"

"Consider coming to Bethel Manor and discuss this with James and allow me to be the mediator."

"How can you be impartial? He's married to your daughter."

"I give you my word, I'll not take either side. I will merely help guide the discussions and see if we can't come to a mutually agreeable solution. Trust needs to be rebuilt and it takes time. But it begins by a willingness to hear the other person."

Patrick turned his back to Fredrick again and murmured, "Why should I do this?"

Fredrick went to him and touched his back. "Because I know you to be a man of God. We both know, hatred eats the soul."

"Let me think about it." Patrick relaxed and looked at Fredrick. "I sincerely appreciate you coming. Forgive my anger."

"You've been hurt. Clare has shared in your pain and has reconciled with James. Why not let God heal your heart and your home, too?"

"I'll try."

Fredrick picked up his coat. "All I ask is you send a note when you're ready to come. In the meantime, Phoebe and her parents, are welcome to stay with us, although I know she desires to come back to you. She loves you."

Patrick tightened his lips and slowly

indicated his agreement.

Chapter Nineteen

George Andrew wailed. Baby Daniel joined George, screeching at the top of his lungs and created a cacophony. Sara stopped hopscotching around the settee and covered her small ears.

Clare bounced George gently in her arms. "We should probably put the children down for a nap."

"Must we? I'm enjoying their company regardless of the chaos. They make me smile." Grace took Sara's hand and hopped a few steps with her, making the toddler squeal.

"Let's allow them to stay with us a little longer, shall we?" Phoebe handed Sara a doll. "Children are precious. It doesn't matter their age." The child stopped moving, put one thumb in her mouth and rocked the pretend baby.

Phoebe cradled Daniel on the settee, as Clare continued to pace with George.

The noise subsided to a slight whimpering from both infants.

"You're such a good mother." Grace sat next to Phoebe. "It's obvious you invest a lot of time with your two and don't pass the children over to staff on a whim."

"I wasn't implying we should give them to someone else when I said they should go down for a nap." Clare's defenses rose and her tone was unintentionally harsh.

"Oh, I wasn't implying you were," Grace replied. "It's just we seem to have help whenever we need, and it makes it easier to use that option."

Phoebe glimpsed at Grace then Clare. A questioning look crossed her features. "One day you'll have babies of your own, Grace."

"Perhaps. Only God knows the future."

"Whenever you decide to marry, I'll be ready to help when you do have children." Phoebe placed Daniel in a cradle.

"What a lovely thought." Grace ran her fingertips over the top of Sara's hair and the child leaned into her. "It would be perfect if we ended up being neighbors and we could bring our children to visit one another."

"That would be quite pleasant."

Grace lifted Sara and settled the child on her lap. "How wonderful your parents decided to stay at Bethel Manor for a few days. What a lovely gathering we're having. It makes these short, dark days tolerable when we have guests."

"I'm grateful they've agreed. They've left to get some things from home but should return shortly. It will be nice to spend time together. They can get to know you also. In fact, I'm looking forward to spending time with you myself." Phoebe pointed at the harpsichord. "Do you play?"

"Not really. Clare has been trying to teach me, but I'm hopeless."

"No, you aren't. I'm not the best instructor. I'm afraid my patience is quite limited. Practice is all you really need." Clare continued to pace and George grew heavier in her arms.

"Shall I give you a few lessons?" Phoebe stepped to the instrument. "It's actually quite simple once you understand the basic cords."

"Would you really show me how?"

Phoebe's fingers glided over the keys and she seemed to slip into a peaceful trance as she played.

Sara slid from Grace's lap and began hopscotching again.

"It's beautiful." Grace joined Phoebe at the instrument and hummed. "You're very gifted."

Clare peered at the two. Her sister-in-law was obviously taken by Phoebe's graceful self-assurance. Could she do nothing wrong?

She looked away. Was she the only one who seemed to struggle with the beauty and talent of this person she'd known her entire lifetime—her best friend?

"Do join us, Clare." Grace gave a short wave in her direction.

"Thank you, but I'm going to take George upstairs and put him in his cot."

Grace smiled and turned back to Phoebe. "Would you mind playing the same piece again, please?"

Clare slipped out, feeling as if she'd never been a part of the party.

+ + +

James entered the sitting room. "Is this gathering strictly for women?"

"You're always welcome, dear brother." Grace grabbed James's arm and guided him to the harpsichord. "You should hear Phoebe play. She's very talented."

"Grace exaggerates." Phoebe blushed and placed her hands on her lap.

"She most certainly does not. I've heard you play, and you are indeed very gifted."

"You're too kind." Phoebe gazed up at him, and he quickly looked downward.

"I've…come…to say your parents have returned. They wondered if you would join them in their assigned room. Abigail will take you to them."

"Absolutely."

As Phoebe made her way to the door, Everett crossed the threshold and skirted around her to avoid a collision. "Excuse me, Miss."

"Never mind. There's no harm done. I've just avoided a collision of my own." Phoebe glanced back at James and departed.

Everett said, "Master Thomas and Master Michael have arrived with a guest and wondered if this was a good time to see the family."

"Indeed it is." Grace clapped and her smile spread from cheek to ruby cheek. "Please show them in."

James chuckled lightly. "Why I think you might enjoy seeing Michael again, dear sister."

She tapped his arm. "Don't be silly. It's wonderful to have this many guests. We've been very somber. Having others with us takes our minds off our loss."

"I'm sure that's the primary reason." He squeezed her hand. "Show them in, Everett. I'm curious as to who their guest is."

"I am as well." Grace glowed with excitement.

Thomas and Michael followed Everett into the room. "We thought you might want to see an old friend."

They moved aside and a nurse pushed in a Bath chair, its folded hood covering the patient.

Thomas collapsed the hood. "Simeon

Quire's been wishing to see you."

James's first inclination was to step back. But he'd long forgiven this man who had tried to ruin his life. "What a kind surprise. And how thoughtful to come when the weather's disagreeable."

Simeon spoke through twisted lips. "I wanted to see you and the family and share in your bereavement."

Chapter Twenty

"Please come in." James shifted a seat away from the fireplace, and the nurse maneuvered Simeon's chair into its space. "We insist you stay until Fredrick returns."

Simeon wiggled his nose as if it itched. His spectacles shifted, and the nurse set them upright. "Thank you, Sister Theresa." He turned to James. "She takes good care of me."

"Why don't you join the other staff downstairs, Sister. I'll have them prepare food for you," James offered.

"How very kind. I could do with something warm to eat."

Michael negotiated his way over to Grace, and she curtsied. "It's nice to see you again."

He tapped his hat and offered a short bow. "And you, miss."

Thomas murmured to James, "I think we've done a bit of matchmaking."

"I'm pleased to see her smiling again. It does my heart good."

"Another romance blossoming within Bethel Manor?" Simeon's crooked lips drew upward. "I know I have no right to enjoy your family, James, but it does me good to see Grace happy. She's such a lovely woman. Kind and courteous."

"She's definitely those things and much more. I'm pleased you enjoy being here." James found he meant his words and perceived a softened heart within Simeon Quire, once his mortal enemy. The man now bore the tenderheartedness of God that Fredrick had demonstrated to him and thus changed Simeon's life forever.

"And where's Fredrick, if I may ask?"

"He's gone to see Patrick Tripp. There's been a misunderstanding and he's trying to sort personal issues with him."

"If anyone can sort another, it's Clare's father. With warmth and empathy. He offered me compassion, a place to stay while I recovered, and provided care by Sister Theresa all the while knowing I'd tried to ruin you and the Shaw name." Simeon's watery eyes seemed magnified beneath his glasses.

"That's behind us now." James resisted the urge to mentally rehearse what he'd endured in Ely's gaol because of this man. It was there he met Matthew, his blind friend who spoke of

God's love in spite of his circumstances. Matthew had changed James's life forever in that unbearable place.

"Well, well, well. Who do we have here?" Fredrick entered and tapped Simeon's shoulder. "What a surprise. I must say you look much better than you did the last time I saw you."

"Due to your kindness."

"It seems you're being well taken care of and that's what matters."

"Because of you, Fredrick. You help everyone, even those you don't know. I understand the children in the Bristol orphanage are thriving because of your generous provisions. Authorities in Ely are seeking ways to emulate the orphanage's success." Simeon's features glowed from the fire's warmth. If the Bath chair weren't beneath him, it would seem as if he weren't physically impaired.

"We wouldn't have known anything about Alpheton Orphanage if it hadn't been for James." Fredrick looked in his direction.

"I've recently received a note from George and Margaret Owen sending their condolences. They have their hands full teaching the children at Alpheton how to read and write, and making sure they're a valuable asset to society," James said.

"There's need for more of their type of care rather than tossing them into workhouses. The cities are bursting with children being abandoned and suffering in those dreadful accommodations." Fredrick made his way to the settee. "We hope to travel again to the orphanage in the spring. They'll need seed crops and we've plenty to offer from our storerooms."

"See what I mean? You're always thinking of someone else's needs," Simeon said.

"And always forgetting about his own. I imagine you've had a long journey, Fredrick, and your discussions with Patrick may have been tiring. Would you like something warm brought in?" James asked.

"Splendid idea." Fredrick sat and crossed his ankles.

James rang for a servant and waited.

Several minutes passed. Conversations halted. Michael and Grace looked around at the others as if wondering what to do.

Simeon shifted.

The room grew silent. Where was the servant? Each bell below stairs was assigned a different tone to designate which room to attend. It was expected the staff would come at once.

"Why is no one responding?" Fredrick's face shifted from cordial to dark and serious. "We seem to be having issues with our staff these days. My coach wasn't ready. Meals have been delayed. I've been ignored when I've asked for aide."

"Jean's left a vacancy. I'm sure it will take time for the staff to adjust." James pulled the cord once more.

"That's all well and good, but I think there's something else going on. I'll see to it myself." Fredrick straightened, moaned as if in discomfort. "Excuse me, Simeon. I do hope you will consider staying with us for a night or two. You've traveled from Ely and I know it wasn't an easy excursion. There's plenty of room in the East Wing."

"I wouldn't want to intrude. I'm sure you want to be alone with your family."

"It's no intrusion having you with us. Besides, you've become a part of our family." Fredrick tromped out.

Thomas cleared his throat. "Fredrick seems somewhat distressed."

"He was hoping to take everyone on a journey right after Christmas. The staff became agitated they wouldn't be able go to their families. But many of them had already had time off before the holiday. For some reason, there seems to be unrest in the ranks and they're taking it out on Fredrick. He's such a generous man and takes any rejection quite personally."

"If I could get out of this blasted chair, I'd take care of those villains myself." Simeon's brows furrowed.

"Fredrick will handle the situation with decorum and grace." Thomas placed a hand on Simeon to calm his distress.

"The trouble is, Fredrick may be

tormented by their actions and won't do anything to reprimand them." James chewed the inside of his mouth. Should he follow his father-in-law and stand up for him or allow Fredrick to take care of the problem on his own?

Yet, he couldn't help but be concerned Fredrick was beginning to look haggard from situations demanding his attention. Add the problem James had incited with Patrick and everything might push Fredrick past the point of no return.

Chapter Twenty-One

Clare passed Phoebe's parents' room on her way to the kitchen.

Giggling escaped from behind the closed door. She paused. No matter what happened to this family they seemed to bounce back.

She started to move forward but stopped when Phoebe spoke.

"Thank you both for understanding. Patrick has been strange these past few weeks." Phoebe's tone grew serious. "There's no reason for him to be this jealous."

Clare waited.

"Are you positive, my dear?" Mary was obviously nearer the door. Her words were clear, yet rigid. Any good-humored nature previously filtering out was now gone.

"What are you implying, Mother?"

"Perhaps you allowed your feelings for James to go too far."

She stepped closer and held her breath.

"I did no such thing."

"Sometimes we allow others into our inner space where they don't belong. You may have allowed James to be exposed to your more vulnerable side. You were lonely. It's understandable."

A pause. Phoebe said, "Yes, maybe I did."

Clare looked back and forth along the hall and moved nearer, her ear almost touched the wood.

"James was lonely, too, with Clare pushing him away because of her blindness." Phoebe's voice drew closer. "Both of them were in pain. She hurt him terribly. And I admit he was susceptible to affection as well. He was confused and broken."

"It could be Patrick does have reason for concern."

"Both James and I realized we needed to consider our spouses. But honestly, we had no intention of letting our feelings get out of hand. I love Patrick. And James loves Clare."

"Why didn't you tell Patrick this in the first place if there was nothing to hide. Or are you hiding something from yourself? Something you may be unwilling to admit?" Phoebe's mother prodded.

"May I help you, miss?" Everett appeared from the opposite room.

"Um. No. Thank you." Clare raised a fist

to the door, as if to knock, until her father's manservant disappeared down the stairs. She leaned in again. What had she missed?

"What about Clare?" Mary asked.

"She's been my dearest friend. But this has caused an estrangement in our relationship. I can tell we aren't as close. She keeps me at arm's length."

"Can you blame her?"

Another long pause.

Could they hear her heart pounding? Part of Clare knew she was eavesdropping yet she couldn't walk away. She didn't want to. She had to know the truth.

"I suppose not."

"How would you feel if she were alone with Patrick under the guise of bringing the children together?" Mary's questioning caused Clare to sniffle and swallow hard. She never imagined Mary would have considered Clare's feelings over her own daughter's.

"I never thought about it that way. You're right...I would have deemed it inappropriate."

"There you have it. Patrick has every reason to defend his home if he feels threatened."

Clare nodded to her unseen audience.

She proceeded on her way to the kitchen, well aware she needed to work on reconciling her envy of Phoebe. Patrick obviously was having trouble processing what had happened.

Supposedly, James and Phoebe hadn't meant to keep their meetings secret. But covert activity, whether intentional or not, was wrong. And harmful.

Arguing floated upwards as Clare headed down the stairs to the kitchen. "What's going on?"

The staff remained at attention. Abigail was nearest the head of the long table used for mealtimes. An empty chair sat at the other end, a reminder Jean was no longer there and in charge.

"Tell me what this shouting's about. It's unprofessional and won't be tolerated. Do I make myself clear?"

The staff nodded in unison.

Abigail curtsied. "If I may, Miss?"

"Yes. Please explain."

"Master Shaw was just here and…may I speak plainly?"

"What is it?"

"Your father left us rather confused. Last time he was in the kitchen he told me to handle things. This time he asked Bertie to take charge."

"Did he ask you to take over, Bertie?"

A young, small-boned girl gave a short nod, eyeing Abigail with fear. Her brown hair was tightly tied in a knot making her adolescent features china-doll-like. Bertie was obviously growing into her uniform, her youthful figure still developing.

Why would her father make Bertie responsible? The girl was inexperienced and still being trained. "I'm sure there's been a slight misunderstanding. Abigail, please keep the staff under control. Finish your meal and get back to work."

"Yes, miss. Thank you." Abigail sneered at the others. "You heard Mistress Clare. Eat and get back to your tasks."

Clare left the kitchen. What was going on with her father? Had Jean's death caused a lack in judgment? Abigail was trained, had been with them for a few years, and Clare wanted her to know she trusted her.

She needed to find her father and determine if he needed to be seen by the doctor. He appeared more tired and frazzled since their trip had been postponed. Perhaps his journey to Willow Field, and the trip to fetch the doctor in abysmal weather may have caused even further fatigue. This decision with the staff had been unsuitable. They needed to decide whether to hire another woman to take Jean's position or allow an experienced staff member to step into her place. Father might not be discerning enough to make a decision.

Clare entered the sitting room. When she'd left to take George Andrew upstairs, Grace and Phoebe had been near the harpsichord. Now Grace was with Michael by the instrument. Thomas hovered with James and Father while

Simeon sat in his chair beside the fire.

"Come in, Clare." Grace bounced over to her and took her hands. "There's been a gathering since you've been gone. We only need Elizabeth, Phoebe, and her parents to join us to make our group complete. Shall I get them?"

"Most definitely."

Grace disappeared and Clare scanned the room. She should be grateful for the assembly, but part of her wanted to finish processing what she overheard in Mary and Daniel's room with Phoebe. The other part of her knew she needed to speak with her father as soon as possible.

Chapter Twenty-two

Clare and Grace were the only two who lingered after dinner finished. Everyone else retired for the night after a sumptuous meal of duckling and roast potatoes.

Abigail had proven herself worthy during dinner, directing the staff and holding fast her position of authority. No one questioned what she demanded and throughout the affair protocol was maintained.

Yet Clare couldn't help notice the persistent wariness on her father's face. His eyes darted back and forth from Abigail to Bertie. His lips had tightened and he spoke little. Father left before Clare had a chance to speak with him. If he decided to come into the parlor with her and Grace before retiring for the night, they could address the staff situation.

"You're simply glowing." Clare sat beside Grace on the settee. Reflecting light from the dying embers danced across Grace's cheek. Clare giggled. "But I don't think it's from the fading heat. You seem quite taken with Michael."

Grace twisted at the waist and regarded Clare intensely. "Do you suppose a woman can find love more than once? Or am I attracted to him because of his unsettling similarity to Braedyn? I'm torn."

Grace's blue chiffon dress refracted the light like soft ocean waves. She had the same delicate features as her mother, Elizabeth, yet had her brother's slight concave cheeks and intense nature. An enthralling combination. It was a joy to see the glitter of excitement shining in her eyes again.

"I wouldn't want him to think I was showing him affection as a replacement for Braedyn."

"And are you?" Clare asked softly.

Grace turned from Clare and looked at the dying fire. "Maybe a little. Michael is different than Brae, though. More introspective and he loves to read. We actually enjoy the same poetry. In fact, he dreams of becoming a writer someday, a news reporter in fact."

"How wonderful. I do believe you're quite enraptured by him."

"He's a dear man."

"But?"

"He can't follow his dream. He has to help send funds to his family by whatever means he can. Writers get paid little."

"How would he hope to have a wife and children?"

Grace tittered. "We haven't gone far enough in our discussions as to bring up marriage and a family."

"It's a question worthy of considering."

"When and if the time comes."

Clare leaned back, stretched out and exhaled. "I relish this time of day."

"Do you? I find solitude quite sad really. It makes me realize how lonely I've been. Even though our guests have gone to their rooms, I find comfort in knowing they're here for a few days."

"Ironic, isn't it? I used to be outgoing, wanting the glitz and glamor of life outside these walls. To be with people."

"And now?"

"Now I'm content to be James's wife. To have his children." She patted Grace's hand. "To be with you. Even if I'm not a very good teacher."

"What do you mean? Do you refer to the harpsichord? That's no reflection on your part. It's my lack of skill."

"I'm not convinced. Regardless, I'm happy right here."

"Ah, but I believe there's a remnant of an adventurer in you. You were ready to go on the trip when your father had originally proposed it."

Clare smiled. "Yes, I was. And I do enjoy the excitement of the unknown. Visiting other places. Exploring another culture. Can one have it both ways, I wonder? Be content at home yet yearn for the adventure?"

"It seems we both have questions this evening. How introspective of us." Grace smiled and placed a hand over Clare's. "I'm extremely thankful James has you. And I have you both. You're such a source of pleasure."

"How kind of you to say." Clare moved her hand and daintily covered a yawn.

"Are you ready to retire?"

"I'd hoped Father would join us but it seems he's gone to bed. It's time we get some rest. I'm not sure what's planned for tomorrow, but there will be plenty of activity around the house."

"I know. Isn't it exciting?" Grace gave a small clap and the two rose at the same time, linked arms, and headed to their rooms.

Grace released Clare's arm and opened her bedroom door. "Goodnight, Clare. Thank you for listening to my ramblings about Michael. Sleep well."

"You, as well." Clare proceeded down the hall. The Longcase clock chimed on the eleventh hour as she passed.

Soft sobs emerged from Phoebe's room, one door down from her parents.

Clare paused. Should she knock?

"I was coming to look for you," James whispered from his opened door, his form shadowed by light coming from the room. "Is anything wrong?"

"No. I'm fine." Clare moved and positioned herself in front of him. "And you?"

He stepped into the semi-lit hall. His musk odor and disheveled hair exuded masculinity. This thin urchin who had come into their lives those many years ago and captured her heart could still create a fluttering desire. It was no wonder Phoebe found him attractive. His kind eyes drew a viewer in and offered a safe place to be one's self.

She laid a palm on his chest and felt the rhythmic beating of his heart. "What are you doing awake?"

"Thinking of you."

"You know I love you, don't you?" she said.

"But I never grow tired of hearing you say so."

"Will you always love me, James?"

"What has caused this pensive contemplation?" He entwined his fingers with hers. "The moment I first laid eyes on you, I knew you were the only woman I could ever love. After all, you were, and still are, a force to be reckoned with." James warm breath drew her in and their lips nearly touched.

"Why Mister Blackwell, I do believe it's about time George Andrew needs a brother. What do you think?"

He smiled broadly, opened the door wide and they entered his room.

Chapter Twenty-three

Slices of morning light painted thin yellow lines along the wall.

Clare tiptoed from James room, snuck into the nursery, gathered George Andrew and slipped into her private chambers.

Sara and Daniel were sound asleep in the nursery, and she wanted precious time alone with George. Before long the rest of the house would waken and activities would disturb any stillness she hoped to find.

In the quiet, water droplets fell from the eaves. The steady music of melting snow lulled her as she cradled her son. The warming sun would soon dissolve the ice completely, and in a few short weeks flowering snowdrops would press their white heads through hard soil and triumphantly pronounce the coming of spring.

George wiggled. Infants were as unpredictable as the weather. One minute they were content. The next, they demanded attention and offered incessant cries of supposed suffering.

Right now, George was at peace. His fully opened eyes were filled with wonder and the smooth cadence of his breathing calmed them both. She held him close and hummed a lullaby her mother had often sung. "Hush. It's time for our little one to close their eyes. Hush. It's been a long day, by and by. Hush. Your mother's heart is nigh. Sleep, my sweet, and close thine eyes." Clare had carried on the tradition of singing the tune since George's birth and had no plans on stopping any time soon.

Rap. Rap.

She moaned. The magic was broken. "Yes?"

Phoebe entered. In spite of her hardship with Patrick, Clare's best friend from childhood was delicate in her appearance and seemed to float as she entered. She had the grace of a princess, and her hair, although tousled, was a golden halo. The only sign of the sobbing Clare heard from Phoebe's room were dark circles rimming her eyes.

"Would you care to join me?" Clare whispered, unwilling to disturb George.

"May I?" Phoebe stepped gingerly into the room.

Clare motioned with a nod to the chaise

"Please. Sit."

"I've come because...I owe you my deepest apologies." Phoebe's shoulder's shook as grieving took hold and she cupped her face.

Clare waited. The dripping outside became a clickity-clack, increasing in speed and volume as if to share in her friend's sorrow.

Phoebe wiped her eyes and nose with a handkerchief. "Forgive me. I didn't sleep well last night. I was hoping I wouldn't lose my composure."

"We've been friends for a very long time, haven't we?" Clare gently moved George from one arm to the other.

Phoebe nodded.

"When my mother died, you were the first person I went to for consolation. Jean was my confidante, and you were my strength."

"I remember it well."

"When you met Patrick and knew he was the man you wanted to marry, we rejoiced together as God had chosen such a wonderful person for you."

"But he's changed. I hardly know him now." Phoebe rearranged her dressing gown. "He seems a stranger and never cuddles the children, never mind showing me any affection."

"Do you recall when we went to Brugge?" Clare smiled slightly. "It was cut short, but we managed to accumulate a great deal of purchases, didn't we?"

Phoebe offered a small smile.

"How Father didn't know I'd left?"

"Yes. I remember distinctly."

"I realized afterwards, I was running away from fears I didn't want to face. I wanted my freedom, but I was also trying to escape the reality of my mother leaving us abruptly. And worried about what I'd do, if something happened to Father too. In my mind, I needed to grow up. Take responsibility for myself."

George Andrew began to wiggle and whimper slightly. Clare rocked. The baby settled. "What are you running from, Phoebe? Fear of Patrick or anguish of possibly losing him for good?"

Phoebe twisted the hankie. Sunlight streamed through the window, caught the top of her head and circled it with a crown. There was a supernatural allure surrounding her. Jealousy's ugly claws began to dig in Clare's heart. *God, please stop these feelings.*

"I almost lost James." Clare murmured, hesitant to speak, her emotions raw. "And much of it was of my own doing."

"If I could relive those months, I would do many things differently." Phoebe lowered her eyes.

"Everyone has regrets. I carry my own basket of remorse in my heart. Perhaps God allows these memories to never forget how our actions impact others. There are many things in my life I wish I'd done differently."

Phoebe looked up at her.

The moment their eyes met, the icy and callous beast of envy dissipated like the snow. Clare could no more hate this woman than she could Jean. Their lives had been entwined for as long as she could remember. She whispered, "I forgive you."

"Thank you." Phoebe dabbed her eyes again.

George's whimpers increased. "Would you mind giving me a few more minutes alone with George before he needs to be fed?"

Phoebe rose, knelt beside the nursing chair and placed a hand on Clare's. "You have always been my dearest friend. Could we start our friendship anew?"

Clare smiled. "I'd like too, very much."

Phoebe walked softly to the door and closed it gently behind her.

Thank you, Lord. God had given her the gift of forgiveness. Clare let her tears spill. Healing came with a price. An injury always left a scar but it was up to her whether she picked at the wound.

She held George a moment longer, rose, and took him to his room. The other children would also need attention soon.

Clare placed the child in the servant's arms.

Father had shown grace to Phoebe in

allowing her to come into their home when he knew perfectly well Patrick was out to harm them. His example was one to exemplify. Whatever they needed to do to show grace and mercy to Patrick, they would offer. After all, he was coming to terms with what he found out. The rest of them had already had time to move on with their lives.

George released a shrill cry telling the world of his need. Wasn't Patrick doing the same thing? Crying to the world his hurt? She stroked George's flushed cheek. Soon enough he would be changed and back to sleep. Hopefully Patrick would soon find his own solace and a resolution would soon follow.

Clare left the nursery and returned to her room. She rang the bell for Abigail to come and choose her wardrobe for the day. Black would be a necessity for a few more weeks, therefore her options were limited. Jean would have never wanted Clare to mourn as she had done for her mother, to hold a grief so long one forgot how to live. Jean had even told her once should anything happen to her, Clare was to rejoice and know peace.

Tomorrow she would wear something with a tiny bit of color to match the changing weather outside and her changing heart within.

Chapter Twenty-four

"Where's Abigail?" Clare pulled the rope again. As a general rule, the maid was quick to arrive.

Her servant rushed in and curtsied. "Sorry, miss."

"You seem flushed. Is everything satisfactory downstairs?"

"Yes, miss. Just hurried. Nothing more."

"How's the staff? No more arguing, I hope?" Clare opened the wardrobe in search of a corset and dress.

"They're fine now you've put me in charge...at least for the time being."

"I need to check with Father, but you seemed to handle last night's dinner with extreme efficiency, therefore I see no need for him to change anything. I'm very proud of you."

Abigail curtsied again. "Thank you. Not everyone's pleased with the arrangement."

"It'll take time for everyone to adapt." Clare paused at the mirror. "I'm sure they continue to mourn Jean." Jean would be more than missed. She would leave a vacant space in their world regardless of who was in charge. "How's Sam?"

"He seems to be in a muddle. One minute he's in the kitchen telling us what to do, the next he's wandering around like he's lost."

"Oh, dear. I've been remiss in visiting. I must check up on him."

"I'm sure that would be pleasing." Abigail crumpled the corner of her lace apron into a small wad.

"Why do I feel like you're keeping something from me? You seem distracted."

"It's just…"

"Go on."

"Well." The maid lowered her eyes. "May I say something? Only I don't want you to misunderstand. It's difficult, that's all."

Clare stopped rummaging in her wardrobe. "I hope you know you can always discuss any concerns candidly with me. We need to trust each other if you're going to be assigned such an important role."

"Part of the reason there's problems in the kitchen…is…because your father is very clear he doesn't like me. I'm not sure why," she gushed, a blush of pink spread over her cheeks. "I never did anything to cause trouble."

"Father likes everyone. What would make you think he doesn't care for you?"

"It's difficult to say, miss. He came into the kitchen once and asked me to do something. I was busy at the time. He didn't give me a chance to finish what I was doing and he stormed out before I could assist him."

"That doesn't sound like Father, whatsoever. I'm sure it was purely a misunderstanding. I must say, though, he hasn't been acting quite like himself."

"He seems troubled. Could it be, he needs to see the doctor? Never mind. I should've never spoken, miss. Please don't tell him." Abigail sniffled as if on the verge of weeping.

"There. There. I won't say anything. In fact, I have concerns for his health as well. I was going to suggest he see Doctor Willard."

"If Master Shaw doesn't trust me, why should the staff?" Abigail released her apron and pulled out three dresses from the wardrobe.

"There's no reason he shouldn't trust you. I'll discuss with him how reliable you've been, and insist he keep you in charge. Now. What shall I wear today?"

Abigail smiled broadly. "Whatever you pick will be a good choice." Her maid reddened. "You're the prettiest lady I've ever known. All the servants around the county agree."

"And you're a dear. I have total faith in your abilities. I'm sure Father will come around and see things my way and begin to rely on you, too."

+ + +

"Why are you being stubborn?" Clare hovered over her father's desk. She placed palms down on the edge and leaned forward.

"That's a treat coming from you. The most stubborn girl in the world." Her father's dimple deepened. "Now, please, let me get back to work."

"It's a matter of pride, isn't it?"

"You're serious? You want me to see the doctor?"

"Yes. For your own good."

"Since when have you become my caregiver?" Her father's brows knitted together and his jaws clenched, his genial nature now buried.

She straightened. "I'm concerned. I'm sure Elizabeth would agree, and James. And there's probably nothing a good rest won't cure."

"I'm perfectly fine. I've no need to see a medical professional."

"But you're pale. Unlike yourself."

"Stop treating me like George Andrew. I *do not* need pampering."

"And I might add, short-tempered."

"I am *not* irritable."

If she were to convince her father to listen, she'd have to try another tactic. Clare smiled and winked. "If you go and see the doctor, I promise to not question your decisions for an entire week. What do you say?"

"What kind of deal is that?"

"Imagine, an entire week without me nagging or telling you I don't agree." She moved to her father's chair. "You'll have sole authority over everything if the doctor says you're fine."

"And if I don't go to see him?" Despite his pale coloring and creases along his forehead, he curled a lip and winked back at her.

She wagged a finger. "Remember who's more stubborn. I'll expect to get my own way no matter what."

Her father leaned back and crossed his arms. "You make a hard bargain. Poor James. I should have warned him years ago."

"I believe you tried. He wasn't convinced."

"I bet he is now."

Clare touched his forehead with her lips and lingered briefly. This man had nurtured her with the tenderness of a nursemaid when Mother had died. He put aside any concern for his own wellbeing and focused solely on her needs. "You know I love you and want what's best." She straightened. "It's time someone takes care of you. After all, you're always looking out for others."

He rubbed a palm alongside his face. "Now that you mention it, I have been feeling a bit tired and out of sorts lately. But if I go and see Doctor Willard, we have a deal. Right?" He put out his hand.

"It's a deal." They shook hands.

Her father turned her palm downward and pressed his lips to the top of her hand. "Thank you, my Clare."

"You're welcome." She headed to the door and turned back. "It's perfectly acceptable for you, for all of us, to grieve our loss. Jean was a dear friend and I know you miss her. Cry if you must, tears are not a sign of weakness."

Father blew a kiss and went back to work.

Chapter Twenty-five

"It's amazing how sunshine can change your outlook on life, isn't it?" James strode by Clare along the gravel path to the stable yard. Naked shrubs and deadheaded rosebushes lined the walkway beside the house, but the sun hit the bricks with a golden shower.

"I'm hoping the sunlight will cheer Sam. He needs a little brightness in his life."

"It'll take time."

"It will indeed. Thank you for accompanying me. Father said Sam seems to be doing all right, but men act differently with each other. They think they need to keep their emotions inside as if speaking about their pain somehow makes them weak."

"I'm a man, I understand." James reached for her gloved hand.

"You do the same thing. But I'm hoping Sam will be honest with us. We're family."

"Does it really do any good to speak about one's suffering?"

"I believe God created us to know love and along with that, to know loss. Surely He expects us to express how we feel about both."

"May I suggest we don't push Sam? If he's willing to talk about Jean, fine. He's a private person, and I wouldn't be surprised if he doesn't handle his sorrow in the quiet of his own home."

Clare squeezed his hand. "What wise words. If nothing else we can share in the joy of Jean. Father loved talking about Mother to whomever would listen. It kept her alive for him."

"You said you wanted to speak to Sam about something else. What is it?"

"I want his advice about the kitchen staff. He knows them because of Jean's supervision, and before I discuss with Father what to do to replace her, I wanted to ask Sam who he'd recommend."

"Is there someone you have in mind?"

"Abigail. She seems quite capable."

James stopped. "Really?"

"You seem surprised."

"There's something about her nature I'm not sure of. Calculating. As if she's always looking for something out of place."

"What do you mean?"

"It's the way she looks at the others. Or

maybe the way she looked at me…"

"When?"

"Never mind. It's not important." When he and Phoebe had been in the foyer, Abigail's sneer had sent shivers up his spine. Speaking to Clare about Phoebe wasn't something he was willing to do. Letting sleeping dogs lie was best in this case.

"Father seems to have issue with her as well. But I want to suggest she take over for Jean."

"Don't you think she's too young?"

"Young women are as capable as mature ones given the right training and supervision."

James shrugged. "I trust your intuition, if you think she'd be sufficient."

The stable block was busy with workers mucking stalls, hauling dirty hay out and clean straw in. Winter kept the odor down but scrubbing away the grime was never pleasant. Horses greatly appreciated pristine enclosures like anyone else.

Clare stopped at the first block and stroked Sentra. "Hey there girl. It won't be long before we take a ride. Maybe in a day or two." Sentra nuzzled her long face along Clare's forearm and neighed.

"Mornin' Mistress Clare, Master James." Sam's smile wasn't as broad as usual. His white tufts of hair poked out at various angles from under his cap, and his whole appearance seemed askew.

"If I didn't know better, I'd say you've lost weight. Look at how your coat hangs on you." Clare put her hands on her hips. "My friend, Jean, would be shocked at how thin you are."

At the mention of his wife's name Sam's smile broadened, although his eyes held the pain of loss. "Yes ma'am. She'd be poking my ribs, counting them and making me eat until I were sick."

Clare spoke softly. "Everyone misses her delicious cooking, but I'm sure none miss it as much as you."

"I don't suppose they do."

"How're the workers?" James stepped in wishing to deflect the overwhelming sadness. "Everyone was up in arms about going home to visit their families. Have their complaints settled?"

"Work's kept us all busy. Too busy to think about anything but keeping up with the animals and farm. Which ain't a bad thing." Sam took off the cap and wiped his brow.

"Don't overdo," Clare directed. "We don't want you getting sick."

"No ma'am. I wouldn't think of it." Sam replaced the cap on the back of his head.

"Sam, you know as well as the rest of us Clare frets about everyone." James chuckled. "She did have a question and wanted your advice."

"Me?"

"I was wondering how you thought the servants were doing in the kitchen now Jean's...gone? No one can replace her, but there needs to be order as it's in a bit of chaos right now without someone in charge."

"I've noticed some untidiness when I've gone in. But I fix my own meals at home now." Sam lifted a shovel as if to begin working. "So I can't rightly say who'd be best."

"What do you think about Abigail?"

Sam shook his head. "I'm sorry, Mistress Clare. I can't speak right nor wrong about her. But she seems a bit cunning."

"I mentioned the same concern," James said.

"Thank you. I'll bear that in mind."

James knew Clare well enough to know she had already made her decision. Speaking to Sam about it was purely pleasantry and wanting him to feel a part of their lives. Abigail was destined to be put in charge. He shivered at the thought.

"Are you cold?" Clare asked.

"No. I'm fine. Shall we let everyone get back to work?"

"Of course. It's been lovely seeing you, Sam. By the way, Simeon Quire is visiting with Thomas if you'd like to come and say hello."

Sam tapped his cap. "Thanks, miss. But if

you could pass on my regards that would be sufficient. I'm not much up to visiting these days."

"We understand. Don't we, Clare?" James took her elbow.

"Yes, but I insist you consider coming for dinner in a day or two. Please? For my benefit? We need to put meat on those bones for Jean's sake. She'd be quite cross if I let you go without eating better."

"Yes, miss. Thank you." Sam's eyes twinkled as he began shoveling muck.

Chapter Twenty-six

Clare chewed her lower lip and concentrated on the next cross-stitch. For the rest of the work to be perfectly aligned, it had to be precise. Elizabeth had gifted her this new needlepoint for Christmas, and it was more complicated than others she'd worked on.

The women of the house had gathered in the warmth of the sitting room.

Phoebe and Elizabeth read. Grace tinkled with the harpsichord keys, playing a lively piece. She was becoming more proficient, motivated by the small encouragement Phoebe had given her.

Clare lifted her eyes, tapped her toes to the music's rhythm and smiled. Women were meant to be in community, and the tranquility of knowing the affection of each of these ladies warmed her heart as much as the sun heated the room.

"Where are your parents, Phoebe?" Clare

asked. "I thought your mother would join us."

Phoebe raised her head. "They decided to go back home but will return later in the day. The time may come when we go to their house from here, and they wanted to prepare a room for our arrival."

Grace stopped playing. "It's wonderful having you with us. How long do you expect to stay?"

"I've no idea." Phoebe laid the book on her lap and gazed out the window. "It's lovely being with everyone, but I miss Willow Field."

"I know you must miss it." Elizabeth put her reading material aside. "I can't imagine not being in Bethel Manor."

"What are the men up to, I wonder?" Grace moved from the harpsichord and went to the window.

"They were planning to go on a hunt. Except Simeon. I believe he was resting while the others went out."

Everett entered. "Excuse me, Mistress Clare."

"Yes. What is it?"

"There's a gentleman here to see Miss Phoebe. Shall I show him in?"

"Who could that possibly be?" Phoebe stood, her brows raised.

"Show him in." Clare gathered her needlework and placed it inside the sewing table.

Patrick entered and bowed slightly. "Excuse me ladies for interrupting."

Phoebe stepped back and covered her mouth. "What are *you* doing here?"

Patrick remained at attention and spoke like an officer to his charge, his tone terse and forceful. "I've come to bring you home."

"I'm afraid I can't go."

He took one marching step forward. "I insist. We can discuss our differences in private there."

"We've tried your approach and it hasn't worked. Until you've come to your senses, I've no plans on returning. In fact, I may be moving with the children to my parents."

"You'll do no such thing." Patrick reached out to grab her arm.

"Please, let's be reasonable." Elizabeth moved between Phoebe and her husband.

"I've not come here to cause any problems. But it's my right to have my wife come when I tell her."

Clare joined Elizabeth. "This is the nineteenth century. Stop with the antiquated ways. Phoebe needs to know she and the children are safe in your home."

Patrick's stern form melted and his shoulders drooped. "You, of all people, would think I would harm those I love?" He looked at his wife. "What lies have you been telling them, Phoebe?"

"I've said nothing but the truth. You've been unreasonable and not yourself."

"You're a traitor to our marriage, and you expect me to act as if nothing untoward has happened? Fredrick asked me to come and speak with you. But it seems it was foolish advice."

"It's not foolish. I'm glad you've come. This issue needs to be settled once and for all," Clare said.

Patrick faced her. His voice broke with emotion. "Clare, you should be as upset as I am over this. How can you be kind to a friend who's been disloyal?"

"There's been no betrayal, only poor judgment." Clare took hold of Phoebe by the waist.

"You can be very naïve. And foolish." Patrick regained his composure. The passion in his voice flared again. "When someone has wrongfully harmed you, trust has been broken."

"Is everything all right, Miss Clare?" Those in the room turned as Simeon entered in his chair pushed by Sister Theresa. "I overheard raised voices."

"We're fine. Thank you," Clare said. "There's been a misunderstanding we need to sort."

"May I help in any way?"

"No," Patrick spoke sharply. "It's none of your affair."

"I'll be going then. Forgive me for intruding. Would you please take me out, Sister?" Simeon's mouth twitched and his eyes wandered as if he didn't know whom to address.

Clare knelt beside Simeon's chair. "Actually, I think you could give us useful insights if you wouldn't mind?"

"Me? What could I possibly offer?"

"Understanding on how to accept and offer forgiveness."

Simeon lowered his eyes. "Sister, would you excuse us. This may take time."

His nurse exited quietly.

"Please sit everyone," Simeon said.

Patrick remained standing, as the ladies took their seats.

"If you wouldn't mind sitting, Mister Tripp. It's very difficult for me to raise my head and keep it there for any length of time. Looking up at you is difficult."

Patrick took the small chair by the fireplace and sat on the edge as if to leave in a hurry should the need arise, his knees moving up and down. "Make this quick, man."

"Because you want your problem fixed quickly or because you have no interest in hearing something to change your views?"

Patrick sat back. "There's nothing you have to say that will change my mind, but have at it. I'm listening out of respect for Clare's wishes, nothing more." He glared at Phoebe.

"I'm a man who held hatred in my heart for many years. Loathing brought me to this place, this chair." Simeon squeezed the Bath chair arm. "I'd like to prevent you from being consumed with your own hostility and keep you from ending up like me."

"I have no intention of being like you."

"I never thought my ways were wrong. I placed blame on everyone else, never thinking I could possibly be at fault."

"I've done nothing fallacious."

"No matter. Will you at least hear me out?"

Patrick crossed his ankles and arms, and waited.

Chapter Twenty-seven

Clare indicated to Simeon with a nod. "Please. Begin."

"There's an old saying how a man becomes without what he allows to grow within." Simeon shifted in his chair. "And I'm a testimony of how allowing hatred to be nurtured in a soul can break a body and spirit. What I allowed to grow in here caused my own suffering." He tapped his chest, stopped and gazed around the room as if unsure.

"Go on." Clare urged him.

"It's because Mister Shaw and James taught me forgiveness I'm here today. It wasn't something I deserved. They had every right to let me suffer the consequences of my actions."

Patrick regarded Phoebe as if urging her to look at him. Her eyes remained downcast.

"James's father..." Simeon glanced at Elizabeth. "Forgive me, miss, if these memories are too painful."

"Continue." Elizabeth wrung her fingers, her lips pursed.

"James's father told the authorities of my thievery when I worked as a clerk at the cathedral. Because of his treachery, I did everything I could to destroy his family. On account of my abhorrence of the man, I nearly caused them all to starve. They had to take James to an orphanage so he wouldn't die from hunger." Simeon choked and faltered. "Because of me."

Clare offered Elizabeth a handkerchief. She took it and dabbed at the corner of her eyes.

"That was only the beginning of my deceit. As a result of what I did, their family was torn apart. When James was reunited with them after many years, I sought to annihilate him too."

Patrick uncrossed his ankles, put his elbows on his knees and cradled his forehead in opened palms.

"There's more."

Patrick looked up, his head tilted.

"Again my inward hatred reared its ugly head when James and Clare were married. I didn't want them happy. I had my spy follow them and unearth whatever indiscretions he could find. Instead, the fool killed Braedyn. I'm sorry, Miss Grace. I never meant for that to happen."

Grace turned away, regained her composure and looked at everyone before speaking, "Braedyn didn't deserve to die. He was a kind and gentle man."

"Neither do you deserve to mourn your loss." Simeon addressed Patrick again. "You see the massive pain I've left in the wake of my enmity." He swept an arm around the room. "I'll never forget the suffering I've imposed when I look at them. Pain caused by my hand." Simeon lifted a fist and slammed it down.

Clare rose and went to Simeon's side. "Now tell us why you changed from hate to hope in spite of being chair-bound."

"Even after everything I did, Mister Shaw brought me into his home, and not only did he have Doctor Willard take care of me, Fredrick offered me tenderness and acceptance. Not that it wasn't difficult to have me here. For each and every one of you."

She leaned down beside him. "But it's what God does. He offers forgiveness even though we don't deserve it. We harbor envy, revulsion towards others, bitterness and a plethora of unacceptable thoughts. It's just we can be more sophisticated in hiding how we feel and not act out what's buried in our hearts. Ultimately, each of us have the same capacity to harm others."

Simeon patted Clare's forearm. "How can anyone offer another forgiveness as you have done?"

"Because God has shown us how. And He's told us the greatest of gifts is to love one other as He loves us."

Simeon looked at Patrick and tapped his own chest again. "And love healed this broken person."

Patrick rose. "Thank you. Everyone has demonstrated the power of absolution by opening your hearts to this man. But I'm not sure I have it in me."

"You don't have it in you. None of us does. " Elizabeth got up and moved directly in front of him. "Do you think I wanted to forgive him?" She pointed to Simeon. "Fredrick had to walk me through my anger and reveal to me my own wrong in holding hatred in my heart. The moment I did, I was the one set free."

"Do you think it's easy for any of us?" Grace stood.

"We're human like you. We know it hurts when someone else lets us down." Clare went beside Elizabeth, placed a hand on Patrick's arm and spoke gently, "But can you honestly say you're free from any guilt? You've never wronged another?"

"No. No one can."

Simeon said, "Remember, we have to look within before we can change without."

"You've given me plenty to think about." Patrick fidgeted with his hat and paused a moment before speaking again, "Now may I have a few minutes alone with my wife?"

Phoebe looked up at Patrick.

"Please?" He whispered.

Clare pushed Simeon in his chair out into the foyer. Elizabeth and Grace followed and pulled the sitting room door closed behind them.

+ + +

"What's going on?" James asked. Fredrick, Thomas and Michael, dressed in hunting gear, entered the front door with him. The aroma of fresh air mixed with earthly odors from their hunt crossed the threshold with them. "Why are you lingering in this area?"

"We've had a long conversation with Patrick." Clare shifted Simeon's chair away from the cold air whisking through the entryway.

"He's here?" James stepped up. "Alone with Phoebe? The man can't be trusted." He took a step toward the sitting room.

Fredrick pulled James's coat sleeve. "You will *not* interfere, do you understand? This is no longer your business. If Phoebe wants us to join her, she'll say so."

James nodded. "You're absolutely right. I've no reason to hinder their conversation."

"Perhaps they're reconciling."

"I pray so." James drew alongside Clare and put his arm around her. "I want nothing more than for them to become a family again."

"Simeon offered a heartfelt testimony of

the love of God and forgiveness you and Father offered him." Clare looked up at James. "It's time for everyone to move on with their lives."

"If Patrick would only come to his senses."

Abigail arrived at the end of the corridor and motioned to Clare.

"Excuse me. There's seems to be something going on downstairs."

As Clare passed the sitting room, she heard murmuring within.

Chapter Twenty-eight

Clare walked alongside Abigail towards the stairway. "What is it?"

"I'm sorry to bother you, miss."

"It's fine. But what's the problem?"

"The girls responsible for the laundry. They don't want to do their jobs."

She followed Abigail down the side stairs to the kitchen and into the scullery. Ceiling-mounted drying racks raised and lowered with pulleys were full of clean linens, and the aroma of handmade lye soaps permeated the room. A large table held several flat irons poised for the servants to press the nearly dried articles of clothing.

One maid swiped her sweating brow and placed a flat iron on its metal tray. "She can't keep up," Abigail whispered. "I've told her time and again she needs to be faster. We're getting behind."

"It seems she's working as quickly as she can," Clare tilted her head towards the maid.

They proceeded out the back entrance to a large courtyard where a lean-to building was kept for laundering purposes. In winter, the doors were shut and a fire kept burning in a small stove for the staff to stay warm during the washing process. A large boiling pot of water steamed the room and added further heat.

A robust young woman, white cap perched on the back of her head, was up to her elbows in suds. She pumped a posser up and down in the large barrel to circulate the clothing.

"Pauline, you must work more," Abigail spoke through gritted teeth.

Clare took Abigail aside. "My mother used to say, a little sugar goes a lot further than a spoonful of vinegar."

Abigail's brow rose.

"In other words, you may be too strict with them. If you speak kindly and with encouragement, they'll work more efficiently."

"Oh dear. I've been too harsh." The girl lowered her head.

"You need to remember people are motivated more with encouragement than with animosity."

Abigail spoke softly, "I'm sorry, miss."

"I'm sure you didn't mean anything by it."

"I'll try harder." The maid sniffled.

Clare observed the robust servant as she shook her head and sneered at Abigail's back.

"Do you have something you wish to say?" Clare asked the woman over Abigail's shoulder.

"No, ma'am."

"Thank you for your hard work. Now, please do as Abigail asks since she's taking over Jean's responsibilities and will thereby be your supervisor."

The woman wrinkled her nose as if a field of cabbage had just been harvested. "Yes, ma'am. If you say so, ma'am."

As they reentered the scullery, the pulley had been lowered and more linen was now stacked ready to be ironed. "You must finish by tonight." Abigail softened her tone slightly but remained firm.

"That's better," Clare said. "Is there anything else you need to discuss?"

"Could we go into the other room?" Abigail headed towards the secure cupboard where silver was polished and expensive pieces kept.

Once they had passed through the main kitchen, Clare turned to her maid. "What couldn't we converse about in front of the others?"

"It's just…"

Clare resisted the urge to stomp her feet and tell the girl to get on with it. Jean would have wanted her replacement to be treated with the same respect she gave all the help. "What do you wish to tell me?"

"It's Everett."

"What about him? Father relies heavily on him."

"I know you don't like gossip, miss. It's…"

"Please. Say what's on your mind."

"As much as I commend his work, he seems to like to share too much with the others. I overheard him telling the other men on staff he thinks your father's unwell and needs care but hasn't seen the doctor."

"He said what?" Clare seethed.

"I thought you should know. I wasn't sure whether to tell you or not as that's passing on rumors. He might have a point about Mister Shaw, but he shouldn't share what's going on upstairs with the others down here."

"You're absolutely correct in telling me. I'll see he's dismissed from his post."

"If I could please say something on his behalf?"

"Go ahead."

"Maybe you shouldn't rush. Let me see if it was a small slip on his part. I wouldn't want him to lose his position on account of me telling you this."

"You're being too kind and obviously trying to protect him."

"Please don't let him go. We all make mistakes."

"If you insist. However, I'll be keeping my eye on him, and I expect you to keep your ears open to any other indiscretions on his part."

"Yes, ma'am." Abigail clasped the edge of her apron and twisted it.

"You might want to stop that nervous habit, especially in front of the others. It sends the wrong message. It says you aren't in charge, that you're timid and indecisive. They need to have confidence you know what you're doing."

Abigail released the apron. "Thank you again, miss. What would I do without your patience?"

Clare smiled. "You'll be fine. We'll work together in getting the kitchen returned to the standards we were accustomed to with Jean. Please get back to your job now and be firm but kind."

"It sounds opposite."

Clare chuckled. "Doesn't it? Think of a parent who needs to teach their children what's right and wrong. Sometimes they need to have discipline and love at the same time."

"I never thought of it like that." The maid reached for her apron to twist the edge then released it. "It's time for me to grow up. Otherwise, how'll Mister Shaw trust me, and why would the others listen?"

"It takes time but it will come. And don't

worry about Father. He's had a lot on his mind recently. It does remind me, he needs to contact Doctor Willard. I wonder what Everett meant when he said he was concerned for him?"

"I'm sure it was nothing, miss." Abigail curtsied. "If you'll excuse me, I must get back to the kitchen."

"You're going to do a wonderful job. Jean would be proud of you. I know I am."

Abigail left, a wide smile spread over her face.

What could Everett have concerns about? Did he know something Clare didn't? She would have to contact the doctor herself and ask him to check Father without the knowledge she had asked his counsel.

Clare rushed quickly upstairs. The sitting room door was ajar and everyone was in the foyer except Phoebe. What had she missed in the few short minutes she had been gone?

Chapter Twenty-nine

James locked eyes with Patrick. Although his mind sped, time seemed to click past with slow deliberation. Candles in the sconces flickered. The pungent aroma of dinner being cooked in the kitchen wafted from below stairs. Simeon cleared his throat.

If Patrick was still in a combative mode, James was determined to set him straight. How could a man feel helpless when it came to those he cared for, yet go to battle and fight enemies on the frontline?

What he wished above all else was for Phoebe to be happy. He had caused extreme pain in her life unintentionally. What would she do if Patrick couldn't find it in his heart to forgive? Would Phoebe and her children be forever in a state of uncertainty?

Clare rushed in and stopped next to James. Both waited, held their breath hoping their friends could reconcile.

He asked, "Have you and Phoebe come to a resolution?"

Patrick looked over his shoulder towards the sitting room. Phoebe joined him, clasped his hand and smiled. "I believe we have."

Patrick gazed at his wife with renewed admiration. The luminescence of a refreshed spirit swept brightly across his face, the weight of the world seemingly lifted. "We've prayed together and asked God to give us hearts of forgiveness as this family has offered Simeon. God graciously answered our prayers."

"It's time for us to move forward." Phoebe regarded Patrick with soft eyes and the skin around her mouth was smooth and relaxed. Tension and worry pinching her face since her arrival now gone.

Sara bounded down the stairs, holding the nursemaid's hand, curls bouncing with each step. Seeing her father, she released the maid's hand, ran to him and leaped. "Dada."

Patrick bent and scooped her up. "My sweet girl, I've missed you."

"I love you, Dada." She sucked her two fingers and leaned her head on his shoulder.

"And I you."

Phoebe patted Sara's back. "We both love you very much."

Sara took Patrick's cheeks between her small, plump hands and squeezed. "We go home now?"

Patrick's lips puckered and he squeaked a reply, "Yes. We can *all* go home."

She let go and clapped, moving up and down in his arms.

"I've something special waiting for you there." Patrick winked.

"You do?" Sara stopped her bounce and beamed. "Wha's it?"

"I've prepared a wonderful surprise."

"Tell me. Tell me."

Phoebe said, "If he tells you it won't be a surprise."

"If he don't tell, I don't wanna go," The child shook her head and spoke somberly.

James leaned back and laughed. Everyone else joined in except Fredrick. He watched from the back corner of the room, the tired expression of a man too weary to rejoice.

Clare, Elizabeth and Grace encircled Phoebe. Hugs and tears accompanied the laughter filling the foyer.

James approached Fredrick. "You should be thrilled. Surely Patrick will rescind any intention of taking us to court."

"I'm sure he will, and I'm delighted at their reunion."

"What is it? You look as if you want to run and hide."

"I'm preoccupied." The creases along Fredrick's cheekbone and forehead deepened like ruts of a newly plowed field.

"What seems to be the problem?"

"I'm hearing of more and more unrest in the kitchen and with the field hands. Something's going on, and I can't put my finger on the problem."

"Can't you ask them directly?"

"I'm afraid they'll close ranks and no one will speak to me. Plus, Everett has been acting rather strangely."

"How so?"

"He keeps insisting something's wrong and I need a doctor's opinion. It's as if he thinks I'm dying and not letting anyone know."

"How odd. Clare's been leading Abigail into taking over for Jean. Once she's more comfortable in the position, maybe the others will settle down."

"Abigail's the other problem." Fredrick motioned James into his office and closed the door behind them.

"How so?"

"I'm afraid I don't agree with Clare's opinion of the girl. I can't convince her Abigail's not suitable."

"She seems capable. Are you're missing Jean so much, you can't be objective?"

"I suppose that's a possibility."

"Why not give her a week and see how she gets on? If she isn't up to doing what's necessary, look for another replacement."

"I don't want to undermine Clare but there's something about Abigail I simply don't care for." Fredrick shook his head. "I'm not normally one to judge another's motives, but—"

"Shall I have a chat with Clare and tell her of your reservations?"

"No. Let's give it time as you suggest and see how things proceed."

"If you're positive?"

James sensed tenseness beneath Fredrick's tight smile.

"May I ask a personal question?" James asked.

"Absolutely. There are no secrets between us."

"Do you think Everett might have justification about your health?"

Fredrick slumped into the chair and drew a hand along his face. "As much as I don't want to admit it, I've wondered myself."

"I've never met a kinder man than you, sir. One who is self-assured, and desires to serve those others."

"Thank you. Puffing up my ego is never what I seek." Fredrick closed his eyes.

"I know. But if it weren't for your kindness those many years ago when you took this ragamuffin out of a makeshift hiding place in the woods, I'd still be wandering the fens looking for my place in the world."

Fredrick opened his bloodshot and weary

eyes. "God had a plan for your life. He continues to do so. Plus, you were meant to be a part of this family. What would my Clare do without you?"

"Thank you. Seeing you bewildered about decisions and how to take care of the staff is perplexing to me. As if you're questioning every motive. Of others and yourself. It's unlike you."

"You're right." Fredrick stood, his shoulders stooped as if he'd aged twenty years while sitting. "I do feel rather tired. Would you mind contacting Doctor Willard and ask him to come?"

Chapter Thirty

Doctor Willard, medical professional and dear friend, had been as much a part of Fredrick's life as Jean. The man's rotund face and congenial smile had always given him comfort, even when Florence, Clare's mother, had passed away.

Fredrick thought he would never recover from the hollowness he'd endured those many years. A vacancy never to be refilled. Until Elizabeth. And although she would never take his first wife's place, she had infused new life into his heart. The mere thought of her brought a slight, inward smile.

"Take a few deep breaths and slowly release them." As Doctor Willard adeptly moved the stethoscope over Fredrick's chest the doctor paused and listened at each inhale and exhale, his brow compressed in concentration.

"What is it? Tell me." Fredrick fastened

his shirt when the doctor finished. "Is it something serious?"

"What has given you that impression?" The doctor stepped back.

"I haven't felt like myself. Others have commented I haven't been acting like I normally do either."

"Is there anything bothering you?" He placed the stethoscope in his brown horsehide satchel and snapped the latch closed.

"Lack of energy and concentration. James summed it up nicely when he said I keep second guessing myself. I'm disconcerted somehow."

"None of that sounds like you. In fact, you do look rather peaked. Losing our dear Jean probably has you under the weather. You relied heavily on her and she was, after all, a member of your family."

A choke caught in Fredrick's throat. "I do miss her. Terribly. The house is not the same, and I don't know how to comfort Sam when I see him. There's nothing anyone can say when you lose someone you love. I remember the well-meaning comments when Florence passed. But the words were empty. Hollow. Comfort eludes the mourner."

"Give yourself time. Sam too. It's okay to grieve. This loss could be bringing up past memories which can cause a variety of complications."

"If you're optimistic it isn't anything

significant, I feel better already." Fredrick buttoned his vest and searched the doctor's face.

"I'm sorry you couldn't take the trip with your family as you'd planned. It would've done you a world of good."

"I'm hoping in a few months we can try again."

"Maybe passing on a few responsibilities and taking it easy might ease some of your stress."

Fredrick jerked the ends of the vest. "The last thing I need to do is rest. I'd go mad sitting around watching everyone moving about. I'm not one to stop."

"Very true. I understand you went on a hunt with the men. How did you fare with the exercise?"

"The fresh air did me good. When we got back home, the activity surrounding Patrick's visit seemed to drain whatever energy I had left."

"Maybe you should limit yourself to one or two major decisions or events in a given day and see how you do."

"If you insist."

"It's worth a try."

"Thank you for coming. You know how much I trust you."

"Even when I made such a grave error with Clare?" Doctor Willard lowered his eyes, his voice subdued.

"You did no such thing. Now who's questioning themselves?" Fredrick clapped the doctor's arm and smiled.

"Thank you." Doctor Willard raised his eyes. "I want you to contact me if anything changes. You're in perfect health but the strain could cause you to become unwell. If necessary, I could prescribe something."

"I'm fine, but thank you." Fredrick opened the office door. The doctor gathered his coat and left.

Elizabeth hovered near the large table, pretending to rearrange boughs in the bowl.

"Were you worried?" He joined her.

"No." Her wide eyes and troubled look told him otherwise.

"I'm fine." Fredrick drew her near and hugged her.

Elizabeth released a soft sigh. "I knew he wouldn't find anything wrong."

"Why your obvious concern then?"

"Because I love you, and I've seen how anxious you've been."

"Thank you. When you're with me, the world is a secure place. I've no worries." He bent, his lips touching her soft, parted mouth. Their bodies tightened together in a forceful embrace.

"Ahem."

Fredrick and Elizabeth quickly separated.

"It seems the doctor gave you specific

advice to help you feel better." Clare chuckled.

"You shouldn't sneak up on your father. It's not...polite." Heat rose up Fredrick's neck.

Elizabeth covered her mouth and tittered. Clare walked toward them, giggling. "It's okay, Father. You're married and I'm pleased you're doing well. I came to check on you. I see it wasn't necessary." She pecked his cheek. "I'll leave you two alone."

"Clare?"

"Yes?"

"Before you go, I wanted to thank you for taking on the kitchen staff. I've had reservations, but I hope you know I trust you impeccably."

"I know you do."

"May I offer you a word of caution?" Fredrick took his daughter's hand.

"Absolutely."

"You know I've always taught you to give others the benefit of the doubt. To help someone become more than they could imagine for themselves?"

"That's why so many love you." Clare winked at Elizabeth.

"But maybe I haven't warned you enough there are also people you must be cautious with. Not everyone's as they seem. You're still young. Naïve."

"Father, I'm a grown woman with my own child." She smiled up at him, her dark eyes innocent.

To him, she would always be his little girl. He remembered holding her like Patrick had held Sara and teasing her with surprises. Those days had flashed by, and now she indeed was a beautiful woman.

"I still want to protect you."

"I know you do." Her brows furrowed. "But who should I be guarded against? Do you have someone in mind?"

He shrugged. "No. I suppose not. I'm only trying to keep those I love from being harmed."

Clare tittered. "You'll never change. And I love that about you as well." She pecked his cheek once more and bounced away.

Chapter Thirty-one

"Shall we go for a stroll?" James asked his gathered companions. "The weather's superb right now. We should take advantage of the late afternoon warmth, check on the horses and see how they've done after the hunt. We rode them quite hard."

"We can cheer Sam while we're there, too," Simeon suggested.

"A wonderful idea. When we get back, we'll share a meal before everyone returns to their homes."

"Agreed." Thomas began to push Simeon's chair, Michael and Grace followed. James and Clare waited a moment.

"Are you coming?" Clare asked Phoebe as she and Patrick lounged on the settee holding hands.

"If you don't mind, we'll stay here. We've

much to catch up on."

She beamed at her friend. "Take all the time in the world."

The entourage gathered their coats, hats and footwear, bundled up and headed outside. Thomas wrapped Simeon securely with a heavy blanket. The path would be semi-treacherous but as long as they stayed on the worn track where others had already walked they would do fine.

"Do you suppose Grace can find it in her heart to love again?" James whispered to Clare as they followed Michael and his sister along the gravel path.

"Like Father, she will someday. Perhaps sooner rather than later." She smiled up at him.

Grace's cashmere wool scarf unfurled from a slight breeze off her shoulder. Michael caught the fabric's edge, and gingerly replaced it, being careful not to touch her.

"Thank you." Grace turned sideways. Her dimple deepened and her cheeks took on a warm glow.

James leaned into Clare and murmured, "I believe Michael's enamored by her, don't you?"

"Would that be such a surprise? His brother loved her. And it seems the two men are very similar."

"I guess the *sooner* has happened sooner than we expected." James laughed and reached for her hand.

Sam exited the stables as they arrived.

The first time James had seen this man on his arrival to Bethel Manor seemed like yesterday. Sam's white, powder-puff hair resembled a pile of snow stacked on his head, and his leathery-lined face was a testimony to many years of hard labor for the Shaw family. Sam's toothless grin had warmly welcomed him, and willingly offered James work in the stalls to make a few coins before heading to Ely. Had five years truly gone past?

James waved. "Hello there. We were coming to see how things are progressing with the animals. I'm sure you've taken good care of them."

"They've had a good rubbing down. Now they're eating and getting settled for the night." Sam spoke with a lifeless monotone.

Clare hugged him. "One of the things Father missed when Mother was gone was having someone to hold. I won't fill Jean's place, but I promise to embrace you whenever I get the chance."

Sam grew teary-eyed. "Thank you, Miss Clare. I was thinking how lonely it is going to an empty house every day."

"We want to invite you to the manor and have a meal with us tonight," James said.

"I smell of muck."

"We insist."

Sam's grin appeared. "Thank you, Master

James. It would be an honor. I'll go home and get a good wash."

"Wonderful. Once we spend time with the horses, we'll head back to the house and meet you there."

It seemed Sam had more of a skip in his step as he headed towards his cottage.

+ + +

James directed everyone to their seats around the large mahogany table with two candelabras brightly lit at each end. Not so long ago the room had been filled with Christmas decorations, boxes with baubles readied for storage. It was remarkable how a few subtle changes could transform a room.

The servants were lined alongside the serving table ready to distribute wine and offer the first service when the time was right.

James directed Sam by the elbow as he hesitated on entering. "Come sit between Fredrick and me."

Fredrick indicated a chair. "Please sit. Thank you for joining us."

"I know my Jean did this every day, and she'd be proud to see it this way."

Clare inclined her head towards Abigail and offered a supportive smile. The maid maintained a professional stance and gave small nods to each of the stewards as an indicator to begin pouring.

James had to admit the girl seemed to

have mastery over the staff. Fredrick obviously had another opinion as he stared at the girl with an expressionless look. What was he thinking behind the non-descript scrutiny?

Soup was ladled into bowls around the table.

For a slight moment, the room became silent.

James sat back and relaxed.

Sister Theresa aided Simeon with the cutlery and draped a serviette across his lap.

Phoebe and Patrick's foreheads touched as they leaned in and whispered a few words.

The Coulter's sat across from them and watched their daughter Phoebe's cheerful expressions with obvious joy beaming across their own faces.

Michael and Grace glanced sideways at each other and offered small suggestive looks.

Thomas slurped his soup, totally absorbed with consuming the food.

This assembly of dear friends created an atmosphere of pleasant tranquility of which James was extremely grateful.

He glanced up. Abigail served Michael, slowly, deliberately. Had she inadvertently allowed her arm to rub his and linger a minute too long? She attended Phoebe and went back to the head of the table behind Fredrick. Abigail eyed Michael. If James didn't know better, the girl's glance had a tint of indecency, as if she longed for Michael to notice her. The look disappeared with a blink and she regained her composure.

James shook his head and focused on the bowl in front of him. He was allowing his imagination to get the best of him. Spiraling steam from the bowl brought with it aromas of mixed vegetables, potatoes and a hint of rosemary.

The first round was completed, and the chatter around the table increased. Clattering dishes being set and picked up became part of the dissonance.

"Would everyone like to retire to the living room?" James asked.

"I'm afraid we have to be leaving." Patrick smiled at Phoebe. "I need to take my family home."

"Of course you do." Clare pushed her chair back from the table. "Let me help you gather the children and their belongings, Phoebe."

"That would be grand."

Thomas brushed a linen napkin across his mouth, catching stray food. "Would you mind if we stayed one more night? It's easier to travel to Ely by morning light."

"We'd be happy to have you." James thumped the tabletop and chuckled lightly. "There are a few others here who wouldn't mind you lingering a bit longer as well." Grace blushed with obvious pleasure.

James glimpsed at Abigail. She watched Michael with lowered eyelids and a slight curl of her lip suggested her thoughts were anything but ladylike. It appeared she found pleasure in Michael staying another night as well.

Chapter Thirty-two

Clare sighed as she poured tea. Bluebells decorated the rim and base of the fine bone china cup and matching teapot, bringing spring beauty into a winter's day.

Heavy grey skies coated the horizon, and billows of lower clouds traveled in waves blocking any hint of morning light. Last night's decorative table with the best silver place settings were now replaced with ordinary cutlery and casual dishes.

She pinched a sugar cube with a pair of small tongs and stirred the concoction. "The house will feel empty after everyone's gone."

"We've been used to having company. What shall we do when they leave after breakfast?" Grace slumped in her chair as Clare passed the sugar bowl in her direction.

James poured tea into another cup and blew on the hot beverage. "What do you think about accompanying Thomas, Michael and Simeon to Ely? We can go to the market, have a bit of a shop and return before sunset."

"May we go? Truly?" Grace's countenance shifted from forlorn to festive.

"I see no reason why not. Things around the house are relatively quiet, and the kitchen staff seems to be somewhat back to its proper routine. Besides, the fields are not ready to be planted quite yet.

"Do you think Father would join us?"

"We could ask him." Grace clapped delicately. "How wonderful if we could all go."

Elizabeth entered the room. Clare's father dragged in behind with dark circles shadowing his eyes. His skin tone matched the grey, overcast sky.

"Good morning," Clare said.

"It is a wonderful morning, is it not?" Elizabeth sat beside her. "Even with the grim sky we can rejoice together over Patrick and Phoebe's reunion."

If Clair didn't know better, she'd question Doctor Willard's opinion of her father's health. "Father, how are you feeling today?"

"I must admit, a bit tired. I can't seem to stoke my proverbial steam engine into gaining momentum." He rubbed a palm along the back of his neck.

"You do look rather drained. Shall I have the doctor come back?"

"There's nothing he can do. I'm sure it's age." Her father lowered himself slowly into a chair as if every muscle ached.

"We were considering going to Ely with Thomas and the others this morning, and we wondered if the two of you would like to accompany us."

"Thank you, but I think I'll stay here. I've letters I need to write and other accounts needing attention."

"The fresh air might do you good." Clare caressed his forearm with a gentle stroke.

"I'll take time and go out and see the field hands. I'll get my fresh air then. Seems there's ongoing discontent among the workers. Sam spoke to me after dinner last evening."

"Perhaps it goes back to them wanting time off to visit family. You might consider letting a couple of staff leave to diffuse the restlessness," James said.

"What a marvelous idea. I'll talk with Sam about a rotation for each to go home."

"If you're positive you won't join us?" Grace's worried look confirmed Clare's own misgivings about her father.

"Not this time."

"You have no issue with us leaving you? I'd be happy to stay." James offered.

"Absolutely not. I'm tired, not passing into the next life." Her father chuckled slightly as if to assure them. "I'd rather you accompany the ladies. You never know what type of vagabonds are begging on the streets, or thugs with nothing better to do than taunt women traveling alone."

"I'll stay here as well. I've notes I need to post to those who were kind enough to visit after Jean's passing," Elizabeth said.

"It's settled. We'll leave in an hour if everyone's ready." Clare rang a small bell and Abigail entered. "Please ask Sam to prepare the carriage and an extra horse."

"Yes, milady. And shall I bring more tea?"

"Yes please."

"At once, milady." Abigail curtsied and left.

"She did well last night, don't you agree?" Clare smiled.

James and Father remained silent.

"I'm not sure what the two of you have against Abigail, but I'm out to prove you both wrong. She'll be the best housemaid, I promise."

James acknowledged the comment with a nod while her father remained unsettlingly passive.

+ + +

Fredrick rearranged papers from one side of his desk to the next. Endless streams of letter writing and financial responsibilities dealing with the manor were the most difficult part of running a large estate. In fact, it was what he detested most. He'd much rather be getting his hands dirty alongside Sam and helping to train the next generation of workers. Not every estate owner agreed with his hands-on approach, but over the years he'd discovered it to be the best way to get jobs accomplished with little push back. Until recently.

He opened the desk drawer and pulled out his pipe. Laid it aside. He mustn't get distracted. If he could work his way through this stack, he'd allow himself the pleasure of strolling to the stable yard.

Abigail brought in a tea tray and placed in on the sideboard.

"Thank you." Fredrick gestured slightly with a nod and returned his attention to a letter addressed to his solicitor.

He glanced up. Abigail remained in his office.

"Is there something else?"

"The ashes needs cleaning." She pointed towards the fireplace.

"You can see to that later."

Abigail stayed in place.

"You're dismissed." Fredrick checked his tone. Getting irritated would do neither of them any good. Besides, hadn't he wanted to help young servants gather confidence in their skills? Clare was trying to follow his example with this girl yet his intuition told him she was not to be trusted.

"In a moment." The maid's cold, calculating eyes were a reminder of when he had gone into the kitchen and she'd refused to help him gather things for Jean. Was he harboring anger over her previous insolence?

"Excuse me?"

"I'll leave shortly. Once I've taken care of the fireplace."

"You impertinent girl. Do you think because you have my daughter twisted around your finger I can't dismiss you?"

"I know you can, sir. But you won't."

"Why wouldn't I?"

"Because you want to give Miss Clare the chance to shine. Like she wants me to shine." The housemaid's face contorted slightly into a mixed combination. Her lips screwed into an odd-shaped grin.

She reminded Fredrick of a child trying to get away with something they'd been told not to do.

"You think you have some kind of power over me? Over her?"

Abigail curtsied. Her wicked smile stayed in place. "I'll go now, sir. Ring if you'd like more tea."

Fredrick remained dumfounded as the girl took her leave. Would Clare believe it if he told her about Abigail's insolence? Her outright defiance and malevolent demeanor? Something needed to be done about this dreadful maid, and quickly, lest her rude and disrespectful behavior spread like a further plague among the servants.

Chapter Thirty-three

"It's a shame the weather isn't nicer." James helped the ladies disembark from the carriage. Although a short set of portable steps had been placed by the door it was easier for him to guide each woman down rather than let her lose her footing on the unsteady, damp treads.

On bright, warm days Ely bustled with activity. Boats moored along the River Lark bobbed in gentle cadence as others passed along the canal. Seagulls swooped into the river's rise and fall as if toying with the dark water. Today, the foamy crests seemed to reach up to the hovering birds and slap them with frigid fingers. People hustled along, their chins tucked in heavy coats and scarfs.

Clare rushed ahead to a lane entering the square where vendors had their wares ready for purchase and traders shouted out prices for goods.

She waved the others forward. "There's still plenty of liveliness in the market. Shall we buy fresh eels to bring home?"

James caught up. "Absolutely."

"On second thought, maybe we should get them last, just before leaving the city. Otherwise we'll be carrying them, and the odor will be off-putting to us and everyone else." Clare wrinkled her nose in mock distain.

"Let's have a quick walk around the town and go into The Bull and order something to eat. I'm sure they'll have a fire going, and we'll be ready for some warmth. Afterwards, we'll come back here." James guided her by the elbow around a throng of buyers haggling over the price of fried eels. Peddlers pushed past with fabrics, vegetables and an odd assortment of commodities.

Space was limited in the market. The narrow lanes leading to and from the square were hives of activity.

Every time James returned to this beautiful city whose reputation was known for one of the largest cathedrals in the world, bittersweet memories swept through his thoughts. This was where he had discovered his roots. But it was also here where he'd been thrown into the gaol because of Simeon's hatred.

He glanced Simeon's way, and the cripple eyed him as if he read his thoughts. A sweep of pain brushed across Simeon's features, and he offered a short nod in James's direction.

James nodded in return. The experience he had undergone was part of God's master plan, similar to the story of Joseph from the Bible. George Owen had often read to the orphans at Alpheton House about how Joseph had been thrown in prison because Potiphar's wife had made false accusations. Joseph had done nothing wrong, yet God had used the incident to form him into a new man. His servant had been humbled and given the gift of interpreting dreams and the knowledge of God's faithful work in his life.

James had walked away from his prison experience with gifts as well, greater faith in God and a deeper devotion to Fredrick Shaw. Clare's father had rescued him from Sheol and an allegiance to Fredrick had been seared into his heart from that day forward.

Michael and Grace stopped at a storefront. Volumes by Charles Dickens were on display in small, neat stacks, their deep red and blue covers a rainbow of masterpieces. Front and center was his infamous *Pickwick Papers*. Elizabeth Barrett Browning's poetry sat beside Dickens' books. "We'd like to stop in here if we may?" Grace asked.

"Please do." James and Clare watched from outside the store window while Grace peered from inside and waved. Michael went beside her and winked.

"They make the perfect couple." Clare sighed.

"My dear, you are the interminable romantic."

"I suppose I am."

Thomas stepped up beside them. "It's time we parted ways. It's difficult to get around with this many people." He directed Simeon's chair toward High Street. "Sister will take Simeon to his quarters. Besides, I mustn't stay any longer. My wife and children will be looking for my return. I'll stop by the market and buy some sweets to pacify for my delay in returning from Bethel." He chuckled, tossed a coin in the air and pocketed it.

James and Thomas shook hands. Clare squeezed the big man, gathered her skirt and squatted besides Simeon. "Please come and visit whenever you'd like. You're always welcome."

Simeon looked up at James. The lenses he wore enlarged his eyes and at the same time magnified a sense of permanent torment in them. "I hope someday we can be together, and I can forget what I did to you."

James held out a hand and the men shook. "What God has done, let no man cast doubt. Besides, what man considers a plan for evil, God uses for good."

"Maybe someday my faith will deepen, and I'll also understand His ways." Simeon released James's hand. Five minutes later the wheelchair bound man, pushed by Sister, rounded the corner and was gone from view.

+ + +

Clare and Grace climbed into the carriage. James worked his way up to sit beside the driver and keep the paper-wrapped fish out in the open air.

"What a delightful day." Clare leaned back against the button-cushioned seat.

Grace pressed her face against the tiny window and waved at Michael one last time.

The driver flicked the reins and gave a short shout for the horses to start the journey back to Bethel Manor.

Grace leaned back next to Clare and closed her eyes, a slight curl drawn along her lips. "It was indeed a delightful day."

"When does Michael hope to visit again?"

Grace opened her eyes. "As soon as possible. But it may be a few weeks as he has other responsibilities to take care of before he can return."

Clare grew serious. "You do realize he's *not* Braedyn?"

"He's a charming man in his own right and will never replace Brae. He misses his brother, too. We share in our loss and love of him which makes Michael even more endearing."

She smiled. "I'm pleased for you."

"Thank you." Grace shut her eyes once more.

A comfortable silence reigned during the ride home.

Although the day had been grey, their time in Ely was exhilarating after being cooped up at home with a constant reminder of Jean's absence. Father would have been cheered up by the city's bustle if he'd chosen to come. Elizabeth would have enjoyed the diversion as well.

Clare jolted awake at the last turn into the estate drive and sat upright. No matter how many times she saw Bethel Manor, she never tired of its spectacular welcome.

The carriage approached the front entrance, and the horses came to a halt. James dropped down from his perch, opened the door and held out a hand.

As Clare stepped down, Elizabeth rushed out of the front door. "Please hurry inside. Your father's quite distraught. He was concerned something had happened to you, and I couldn't calm his unease. He needs to be reassured you're fine and back home."

"Where is he?" Her gaze swept the house as if she could locate his whereabouts through walls of stone.

"In his private chambers. Make haste, my dear. I'm afraid nothing short of your presence beside him will relieve his distress."

Clare sprinted inside. Whatever could be

wrong to have filled his mind with such dreadful foreboding? "Father? I'm coming!"

Chapter Thirty-four

"I'm home." Clare dashed into her father's room.

As soon as he saw her, he stopped marching across the silk Oriental rug and rubbed a kerchief across his brow. "My dear, where have you been?"

"You were aware we went to Ely. Remember?"

Her father shook his head as if waking from a dream. "I was concerned."

She led him to the bedside and urged him to sit. "I'm fine. Why are you so distressed?"

Elizabeth waited in the doorway tightly winding a spiral of hair draped along one shoulder and chewed her lower lip. James and Grace lingered behind her.

"I thought you'd gone." He rubbed the kerchief along each temple and under his nose. "Like you did last time. To Brugge."

Clare touched his forehead. "You may be running a fever. You're drenched with sweat."

Elizabeth stepped inside the room and released the lock of curl. "I tried to tell him he was feverish. But he was in anguish and wouldn't listen."

"James, please go and get Doctor Willard. Something isn't right." Clare guided her father's legs onto the bed and propped pillows behind his back and neck.

Grace joined Clare and Elizabeth. "I'll get some cool water and cloths, shall I?"

Clare nodded. "Yes, please."

Father reached out and clutched her hand. "I'm fine. You know how I worry about you, my dear."

"You've no reason to be concerned I'll leave and not come back."

His eyes welled. "What's the matter with me? I feel unable to control my emotions."

"Let's see what the doctor has to say. I'm sure you're just overwrought."

Grace returned with a small basin and clean cloths.

"Shall I have Abigail bring you some tea?" Clare squeezed water out of a cloth and dabbed his forehead.

"*No*. I don't want the girl anywhere near me." He gently pushed her away and began lowering his legs in obvious distress.

"There's no need to get upset. Please lie

back. I won't ring for her. Elizabeth can get you something warm to drink. Would you prefer her instead?"

Elizabeth's worried countenance changed in an instant. Her eyes expressed relief at being assigned a task. "Yes, yes. I'd be glad to go make you something. I'll see to it at once." She patted his leg through the plush coverlet and scurried from the room.

He leaned back and murmured. "She mustn't be allowed…"

"Allowed to do what?" Clare leaned in closer.

"She mustn't…"

"Are you speaking of Abigail? Elizabeth?"

Her father slid further down the bed and stopped mumbling.

Clare glanced at Grace. "What do you suppose happened while we were gone for the day?"

"I can't imagine. Elizabeth was here but perhaps she was busy elsewhere with little George."

"I've never seen him this worked up except the time I returned from my trip many years ago. But why would he relive that particular memory now?"

Elizabeth returned with a tray and placed it on a dresser while Clare wiped her father's arms and face with the cool cloths.

"You should try drinking some tea." Elizabeth lifted his head and helped him sip from the cup.

Her father reclined and finally drifted off to sleep.

Clare pulled a chair nearer the bed and sat. "Rest well, Father," she said in a low voice and muttered a prayer.

The Longcase in the hall chimed upon the hour. Time passed slowly. Surely James would return soon.

Abruptly, the chamber door opened. Clare jumped to her feet.

James strode in, his breaths coming in quick spurts. "I rode Sentra hard and fast. The doctor should be here shortly."

Clare took James aside and allowed a few minutes to pass for him to catch his breath. "It's the strangest thing. When I mentioned Abigail, Father became further agitated. I can't imagine why."

"If he's running a fever, he's probably delirious and not thinking clearly."

James approached the bedside. "He seems to be resting quite comfortably now, thank God."

Clare reached for James's hand and whispered, "I'm frightened."

+ + +

"What could possibly be taking the doctor such a prolonged time?" James opened his pocket watch. "He should've been here by now."

"I was wondering the same thing." Clare leaned on the windowsill and peered out. "I would've expected him to have arrived. I'll go downstairs and see if Everett could have Sam send someone else to fetch him."

"Shall I go?" James offered.

"Thank you. Father has calmed down and I need a short reprieve." Clare started toward the door.

Everett appeared from the hallway carrying a silver tray with a note. "Excuse me, Miss Clare."

"What is it?"

"A message was received from the doctor." Her father's manservant presented the silver tray.

"How odd." She lifted the letter, tore the seal and read aloud. "I'm pleased to hear the news about your father. Since his health seems to have rapidly improved, I will wait until further notice to come to his aide."

"What does that mean?" James took the paper and mouthed the words.

"Why would he think Father was no longer in need of his services?"

"I'll go and bring him back myself. We'll figure out how this miscommunication has occurred."

+ + +

"Thank you for coming." Clare moved

from the bed and greeted the doctor.

"I'm sorry I didn't come sooner. When I received word he was fine, I assumed you were no longer in need of my services. I should've come regardless."

"I'm confused. What gave you the idea Father was better?"

"I received this note with the Bethel Manor crest and assumed one of you sent it after James had come." He drew a note from his bag.

"Who could've sent it?" Clare reached for the letter. "Everyone was here looking after Father."

"I've no idea." Doctor Willard made his way to the bedside and lifted one of her father's eyelids. "What's happened here? He was fine when I checked on him yesterday."

"I found him wandering around the house calling for Clare," Elizabeth said. "I managed to get him up to his room but he wouldn't settle until she arrived back from Ely."

"This is quite a strange turn of events." The doctor placed two fingers on her father's wrist. "His pulse is extremely low. He needs plenty of fluids." Doctor Willard stepped back. "Strange. Very strange indeed. I recommend fluids and plenty of rest. I'll also prepare some herbal medication that will help with the fever. It's imperative we keep an eye on him."

"Shall we set up the spare room?"

"Yes, please. I won't leave until I see an

improvement."

Clare released a loud sigh. "I'm grateful for you. I know he's in good hands and will be back to himself in no time."

Doctor Willard merely closed the latch on his satchel and remained silent.

Chapter Thirty-five

Clare cooed at George who sat perched on her knee. With both hands clasped tightly around his middle, she gently bounced him. His screeches of pleasure made her giggle.

She rubbed her nose across his. "My precious one, I love you."

George's large eyes mirrored James's, but he had her dark curly hair already forming into unruly ringlets. He pumped up and down, his arms swinging in cadence.

"You do tire me so." She chuckled, rose and carried George to his cot beside the window. He could peer at the light glistening off dewy spiked holly leaves and bright red berries delicious looking enough to eat.

A horse passed by the window, its rider moving in practiced measure as it proceeded along the gravel path. "I believe you have a visitor, Grace."

"Someone for me?" Grace rose from the harpsichord seat.

"Yes. Michael."

Grace pinched her cheeks and generated a rosy-red. She pressed the front of her dress to make herself more presentable to a male caller. "I wasn't expecting to see him this soon."

Michael's large, red mustache shifted upward when he dismounted and saw Grace through the window.

"It's obvious he's missed you. Look at that smile."

Everett escorted Michael into the sitting room.

Clare said, "Do come in. How wonderful to see you again."

Michael bowed at the waist. "Miss Clare, we heard your father was unwell and were wondering how he's getting on?"

"Thank you. He's much better now he's had a few days' rest. The doctor has allowed him a short time out of his room, so he's taking a stroll along the hallway to regain his strength."

"Ahem." Michael rolled his eyes upwards and glanced at the ceiling. "Well, that's good news indeed. I'll pass it on to Thomas and Simeon. I guess I'll be going now."

"Are you positive Father's health is the only reason you came?" Clare teased.

Michael blushed and his hair coloring blended with the red hue rising from his neck and across his cheeks.

"Why don't you stay awhile and visit with Grace and me? I'm going to take George to Father as the child always cheers him up. He's the perfect medicine for his weary soul."

"I'm not disturbing you?"

"Of course not. Please take a seat on the settee. Grace, why not sit next to him?"

"But that's where you were resting." Grace lowered her eyelids and turned a bright pink.

"I'll sit in this chair by the fire on my return." Clare tapped the back of the seat and smiled. "You two enjoy your conversation while I take George out."

She resisted the urge to watch the two nattering as she scooped the baby out of his cot and left.

+ + +

"What do you mean you left them unescorted?" James started to rise from Fredrick's desk chair. "Do you think it's a good idea?"

Clare patted the air. "Don't worry. Grace and Michael will be fine. I won't be gone long. I merely wanted to give them some privacy."

"If you're certain?"

"They have little time together as it is. Besides, he may want to ask Grace if he has permission to court her. Wouldn't that be lovely?" Clare gazed skyward, her palms together in mock prayer.

James smiled. "If you say so."

She circled the desk and joined him on the other side. "How's the paperwork going? I know Father appreciates everything you're doing to take some of the pressure. I don't understand why he's found it difficult lately. He's always loved his work."

James patted the top of the desk. "I'm sure he'll be back here in no time. For now, I'm happy to help. Besides, it's nice for him to have George's affection instead of a constant stream of bills and letters needing attention. I did have one question about a particular situation though. Do you know where he's gone?"

"He and Elizabeth decided to bundle up George and take him outside for a stroll. They had him wrapped so skillfully all you could see were his chubby cheeks and bright eyes. He charms them. I'm afraid he's going to grow up quite spoiled."

"Being spoiled is fine until he's older. As he ages, he might become unmanageable." James's smile increased.

"They mentioned they would go and visit Sam. Part of Father's healing will come when he and Sam can be together without strained emotions and inability to know what to say."

"Once your father's stronger, we should begin talking again about our trip. Making plans would occupy his mind and give him something positive to focus on."

"I didn't realize how much the toll of Patrick's threatening to take him to court, the loss of Jean, and the unsettled atmosphere with the staff was taking on him."

"It's been a challenging time but give your father the benefit of the doubt. He's stronger than we realize."

Clare cupped his cheek. "Thank you. I needed to be reassured. Now I can return to those in the sitting room and act as chaperone."

He pressed his lips to her palm. "A fine chaperone you make."

+ + +

Clare returned to the sitting room as Abigail entered with a tray of tea and biscuits and set them on the three-legged table nearest Michael.

The maid poured two cups and served him and Grace.

She turned to Clare. "Shall I pour you some, miss?"

"No, I can do it myself. Thank you." Clare adjusted the mahogany fire screen, with its needlepoint front, to protect her face. Elizabeth had sewn the beautiful peacocks on it as a gift.

Abigail rearranged pillows and aligned the curtains bringing streams of light across the floor and creating an arched halo behind the two on the settee. She loitered behind Clare, made some rustling sounds and retreated from the room.

Michael finished his tea and rose. "I suppose it's time I left for Ely."

"Must you go so soon?" Grace stood.

"If it's all right with Clare, and…you, I-I'd…like to come and see you again…very soon."

"Indeed. It would be a pleasure to see you more often." Clare smiled and rose. "I'm sure Grace would agree."

"Yes. That would be lovely." Grace practically shimmered with excitement.

As Michael left, Grace turned to Clare. "How very odd."

"What? I thought you were having a pleasant time?"

"Not Michael. Abigail. She appears quite enamored with him, and I would say seemed rather bold in her behavior. I was certain she touched his knee when she gave him his tea."

"What could you possibly mean? I didn't observe anything untoward."

"Maybe it's my active imagination." Bewilderment flashed in Grace's eyes. "It could be I'm a tad sensitive at the moment. After all, the handsomest of men has asked to court me."

Chapter Thirty-six

"I feel alive again."

Fredrick inhaled and exhaled deeply as he pushed the perambulator. Its seat jostled with each jerk of the wheels as they rumbled over the pebbles. George sat upright, oblivious to the uncomfortable ride, and made gurgling noises as if chattering with wood pigeons nestled in overhead tree branches.

"You're much more like yourself." Elizabeth took hold of the crook of his arm with her left hand and carried a small bouquet of dainty snowdrops in the right.

"I don't know what came over me, but it's as if horse blinders have been removed from my view, and the world is a grand place once more."

"I'm thankful you're well enough for a walk. Fresh air always does one good."

"Change is in the air. I feel it in my bones. Winter will soon lose its tight grip."

"Now I know you're feeling better. Always the optimist."

Elizabeth's tinkling laughter was a sweet sound, blending with George's babbling, made Fredrick's heart swell. Thank you, Lord, seemed insufficient in how grateful he was for renewed strength.

"It's about time I saw Sam again. I haven't spoken to him since he came to dinner one evening before my health turned for the worse."

"It was a strange turn of events."

"I can't understand what happened. One minute I felt relatively fine, especially after the doctor had given me a full examination. Then my energy drained and I was unable to focus. Actually, that's not really a good description. I felt somewhat disoriented, and a bit paranoid, which is unlike me."

"I don't understand what happened either. I'm grateful it seems to have passed. Sam will be delighted to see you."

"As I will be to see him."

"I hope he'll enjoy these flowers. I'm sure he misses a woman's touch."

"Jean was definitely the one who added color to his life. We must have him over more often to prevent him from spending too much time on his own."

Elizabeth squeezed his arm. "Let's invite him tonight, shall we?"

Arriving at Sam's cottage, Elizabeth used

the doorknocker to strike the front entrance.

"What a surprise. Do come in." Sam's tattered jumper was misbuttoned giving his stance a rather lopsided effect.

"We wanted to stop by to deliver flowers and see how you're faring." Elizabeth showed him the bouquet.

"How kind." He opened the door wider. "You're welcome to come in, but there's no guarantees of its tidiness."

"No need to worry." Fredrick lifted George from the pram and passed the child over to Sam. "George doesn't mind a bit."

Sam held the child at arm's length as if not knowing what to do.

"He won't bite you." Fredrick laughed.

Sam stepped backwards to allow them entrance and cradled George closer. "It's been a long time since I've held a wee one."

Fredrick grew serious. "You and I've both needed something to alleviate our pain from losing Jean. This baby's laughter has been a healing balm for my soul. His joy can help with your loss as well."

George reached out and grabbed Sam's snowcapped hair, gave a gentle yank and squealed.

Sam smiled. "Well lad, if we're going to be friends, we need to come to an understanding. My hair's mine."

+ + +

Clare took George from Elizabeth and untied his cap. "Well, it looks as if you've had a fine time out, young man."

Her father took off his own coat, handed it to Everett and helped Elizabeth remove her cape. "We had a delightful time with Sam. He's going to make a wonderful uncle to this boy." He pinched George's rosy cheeks. "When we left, Sam was smiling from ear to ear."

"I'm so pleased. It's time for George's nap, though. Shall I ring for something to warm you before I have him laid down?"

"Elizabeth and I can take care of the refreshments."

"It's no issue to have Abigail bring something into the parlor."

Her father's face clouded. "I'd prefer someone other than Abigail."

"But she's perfectly capable." Was it possible Father still dealt with delusions? First his concern over her trip to Ely and now this continuous obsession with her maid. Both issues were out of character.

His lips formed a firm line. "I'm sure she is, but you and I need to discuss her position later on."

"Don't you think you may still be recovering from your illness and can't be impartial right now?"

"As I've said, we'll discuss this further when we're able to speak without interference."

He inclined his head slightly towards Everett's back as the man left the foyer.

Clare made her way up the staircase and down the corridor to the infant's room. The nursemaid took George and readied him for a nap.

As she reentered the hallway, Abigail walked towards her and curtsied. "Miss, I see Master Shaw has returned. Shall I prepare some tidbits before dinner is served?"

"It's not necessary. It seems you're busy with other duties. I'll see to it."

Abigail picked up the corner of her apron. "I'm sorry, miss, if I've done anything wrong."

"What gives you that impression?"

The girl shrugged and wiped the tip of her finger under her eye. "It's nothing, miss. I'm sure I'm being a silly girl."

What could Father possibly have against this insecure waif? She seemed to be trying hard and whenever asked to do something she immediately saw to it. "You aren't being silly. You just lack confidence."

Abigail straightened, hands by her side. "Thank you, miss. I don't know what comes over me. I get nervous serving Master Shaw and the others. I'm sure they must think I'm incapable of doing anything right."

"They think no such thing."

The girl stammered. "Are you certain I can't bring something to the others?"

"For the moment, let's leave things as they are. I was going to the kitchen anyway. Finish what you were going to do and begin the preparations for our meal. That will be sufficient. May I suggest you be on your best behavior, too? Remember there are others still deciding who shall replace Jean."

Abigail pinched her skirt with forefingers, bent her knee and lowered her eyes. "Yes, miss. Thank you, miss."

She gently touched the girl's shoulder. "Don't forget I believe in you no matter what anyone else says or thinks."

Chapter Thirty-seven

The kitchen windows misted with condensation and dripped long streamers of sweat from their lofty tops down to the sills. Throbbing heat from the stove and fire burning in the grate kept the kitchen warmer than any part of the house.

Servants maneuvered methodically around the room. No conversations were taking place and each seemed to be in a world of their own. When Jean had reigned here there was always a lively buzz of chatter and lighthearted interaction among the staff.

"My, my. You're a busy lot," Clare said cheerily, in hopes of lifting the rather grim atmosphere. "Jean would indeed be proud."

They nodded in unison like a group of militia in charge of the city gate.

She leaned over the shoulder of a maid who was furiously chopping. "Tell me what you're working on here?"

"Onions and parsnips need cuttin' perfectly." The girl wiped her brow with the back of her hand.

"Surely you can stop for a minute? You look quite exhausted."

The maid placed the sharp instrument down and glanced around furtively.

"There's no need to be nervous. You're doing a fine job."

"Thank you, miss."

Abigail marched in and spoke tersely, "Why are you wasting Mistress Blackwell's time?"

Clare frowned. "I'm afraid I was the one who interrupted her from her chore. We chatted for a few moments, but I'm sure she'll get her work done in plenty of time."

Abigail softened her tone. "Of course, miss." She waved a hand to encompass the entire staff. "You can all take a few minutes while I speak with the Mistress."

A scullery maid set down the cutlery she'd been drying, and the manservant abandoned a silver urn with the cleaning cloth still wrapped around its handle. Servants shuffled out of the room, some looking back at them expressionless.

"They don't seem very happy," Clare said.

"It's Jean. They moan about how it isn't

the same as when she was here.

"I suppose they're still mourning."

"It seems if I jest with them, they try to take advantage of me or think I'm not honoring Jean's passing."

"Don't take it personally. I'm sure they'll come around, and you'll have opportunities to show them your gentler side."

Abigail welled up. "How can I ever say thank you enough, miss? You and your family are such a godsend. Miss Elizabeth is very kind to me, too. I never knew my own mother. I was left in an alley, wrapped in paper like a piece of rubbish."

"Oh, dear. I had no idea."

Abigail rubbed her eyes. "I was taken in by a family, but they had seven of their own and left me to fend for myself. I've never really known...love."

"You poor dear. Did you know Master James was raised in an orphanage in Bristol?"

"Why, no milady. He seems gentrified, if you don't mind me saying so."

"He'd be quite pleased to hear you say so, I'm sure." She smiled. "You see? You have plenty in common with our family and makes you an even better candidate for this job."

"Miss, you're wonderful to treat me with such kindness. No one's ever shown me patience. In the past, I was whipped when I didn't do what I was told." Abigail caressed a scar running along her right elbow.

"You mean to say you were beaten?" The heat in the room seemed to close in on them and Clare felt slightly faint. No child should be subjected to torture.

"It was difficult at first, but I learned to ignore how much it hurt."

"You poor, poor thing." Clare's eyes filled and the misted windows blurred. This was even more reason to insist she have this position. Abigail had potential, yet she didn't even see it in herself.

"You're too kind. Shall I have the staff return and finish their work?"

"Do what you deem best."

The entourage of servants huddled outside the back door, some puffing on cigarettes, grumbled and returned to their stations.

How in the world would they ever get back to the secure atmosphere of Jean's presence? Was her influence a passing fancy? Maybe they would never find another who could demand allegiance and the finest work while offering encouragement at the same time.

Clare gathered a tray to deliver to the parlor for her father and Elizabeth. Walking away from the kitchen was like leaving a morgue. Quiet unease and cold temperaments did not bode well for a house to run effectively. How could she aide Abigail? She daren't ask

Father for his assistance. Perhaps Elizabeth could give her some helpful hints.

She brought the tray into the sitting room. "Where's Father?"

"In his office. James had a question for him." Elizabeth held a pad of paper and several pencils and sketched a few lines.

"Ah yes, he mentioned he needed to speak to him about something."

"He'll return momentarily."

"Shall I pour you some tea?"

"I'll wait for Fredrick. Thank you."

Clare poured herself a cup and sat beside Elizabeth. "What are you working on? You're extremely gifted. You sew and draw and do an abundance of creative things. Where did you gain your training?"

"Seems strange for a woman of such lowly estate, does it not?" Elizabeth's warm gaze showed no offense.

"Oh dear, that's not what I meant."

"I'm sure it wasn't. But I'd be curious if I were you."

Elizabeth's work was impeccable. A quick sketch of Clare's father caught the strength of character in his profile and square jawline. "You don't mind I inquired?"

She patted Clare's knee. "Of course not. My mother came from a well-to-do family. They were merchants in London. Unfortunately, she met and fell in love with my father who was quite charming. However, he was a gambler and lost my mother's inheritance."

"How dreadful."

"It was quite devastating, yet she found ways to keep our family intact and to teach me the skills every genteel woman should know."

Clare sat back and perched the teacup on her lap. "I was speaking with Abigail and she told me about her upbringing. It was quite dreadful."

"I'm sorry to hear that." Elizabeth picked up another pencil and focused on the paper as she shadowed the background behind her husband's profile.

"It seems she was treated very badly."

"We each must come to terms with our lot in life, don't we?"

"I suppose so. But I'm determined to help her."

Elizabeth stopped drawing, scrutinized her work and turned to Clare. "Be careful. Sometimes a sweet spirit like yours can be taken advantage of by a questionable character. I saw it happen with Mother by my father."

"Are you saying you don't trust Abigail either?"

"I'm not saying any such thing. I'm merely offering you a cautious word. However, it could be she's not what she appears."

"I concur. She's not one to be trusted." Clare's father had entered and waited by the door, his shadowed contour exactly as Elizabeth had captured on paper.

Chapter Thirty-eight

"The man's rather infatuated, wouldn't you agree?" James nudged Clare at the entrance of Bethel as Michael handed the reins to a stable hand and strolled in their direction.

"What makes you say that?" She chuckled.

"Wasn't he here a few days ago under the guise of checking up on your father? Then asked permission to court Grace. He's wasting no time."

"Indeed."

Michael made his way to them. "Luck of the Irish mornin' to ya both." He tapped his cap. "Tis indeed a glorious day, is it not?"

"You're acting quite merry this morning. I can't imagine what's caused this increase in joviality." James teased as he guided Michael into the foyer.

"Let me go and get Grace, shall I?" Clare

pecked Michael on the cheek. "Don't let James bother you. He's envious of your courting Grace and wishes he were back in those days."

"Not true." James grabbed her arm as she scurried to leave, laughing and trying to avoid his clutch. "You were a minx when we met. I'll never forget how difficult you were."

"And you were a hardheaded lad." She teased in return, patted him gently to release his grip, went up on her tiptoes and brushed his wayward curl aside. "I took pity on you."

He reached around her waist and drew her close. "We shall discuss your behavior later."

"Yes, sir." Clare dropped from her tiptoes and waved slightly as she headed upstairs, giggling as she went.

"I wish to have as wonderful a relationship with my wife when I marry." Michael followed James into the parlor.

"Clare and I have had our difficulties, but when God is in the center of a marriage challenges can be worked through."

"Wise advice."

"If you'll excuse me, I've work I need to attend to, but Grace shouldn't be long. On second thought, she's a woman and might take longer than a man could ever imagine." James gave a knowing grin and reached out his hand.

Michael shook it, smiling in return. "I'll be fine waiting near the fire. It was a nice day for a ride but there's still a chill in the air."

+ + +

Grace practically skipped down the steps. It seemed her feet didn't touch the floor as she made her way towards the parlor. Life was worthy of living again. Everywhere she turned, colors burst with newness. Even grim wintertide couldn't persuade her to complain. She stopped, smelled and caressed the newly clipped sprigs of pine with tiny cones draped over the large bowl.

She swirled from the table, her skirt swinging in a small circle around her feet and headed to the room where Michael awaited.

As she opened the door, Abigail rushed past and nearly knocked her over.

"What was that all about?" Grace approached Michael whose features were taut, as if displeased.

"What an ill-mannered girl." He rubbed the top of his head and drew the palm along his neck as he exhaled a small expletive. "Sorry. It doesn't do any good to lose my temper."

"What did she do?"

"I'm ashamed to say. It could be I misunderstood."

"Was her manner inappropriate in any way?"

"Not initially. She came in, asked if I needed anything, and when I said 'no' she turned to leave."

"Sounds innocent enough. Yet you look vexed."

"I had peered out the window, and the next thing I know she was standing beside me as if ready to reach out and touch my arm."

"What an impudent girl."

"It was a bit alarming and unexpected."

"Now you mention it, I spoke to Clare the last time you were here and told her I thought Abigail's actions were inappropriate."

"I recall it myself. She smirked at me rather suggestively as she was leaving, but I thought maybe I misinterpreted her expression."

"Did she do something else this time?"

Grace waited as Michael paced a few steps and turned towards her.

"I hate to even mention it. She made insinuations about you. Said you are not who you pretend to be. Your behavior with other men is well known among the staff."

Grace held her warmed cheeks. Her stomach cramped. She feared losing control and becoming sick.

Michael rushed up to her and took her hand. "You know I didn't believe a word she said. When I called her out on it, she explained I misconstrued what she meant. She began to sniffle as if to cry. When you arrived, she ran out."

"The Jezebel!"

"Now, now. Let's not lose our tempers." Michael teased as he led her to the settee. "We've little time together let's not waste it on an imp."

"Be assured, I'll be mentioning this to Clare. For some reason, she seems to think the girl's an angel. Fredrick insists Abigail shouldn't stay in the house in any position, but I'm not sure why. Now I'm beginning to understand."

"Let's speak of something else, shall we?" He released her hand.

"Certainly. Please tell me how your family is doing and what news you've received from Ireland."

"Speaking of my family wasn't what I had in mind."

"Oh, dear. What would you like to discuss?"

"Would it be deemed too unsuitable to ask you how long we should court before…well, before we discuss marriage."

Grace blushed. "I've no idea."

Michael rose and leaned against the mantle. "I watch Thomas with his family and I envy what they share. When I come here and see Fredrick and Elizabeth and Clare and James, it seems unimaginable I could have such an affinity with another."

"They do indeed have special bonds."

He held out both hands and helped her to her feet. "I look forward to the day we can share in the same way."

"As do I. In the meantime, we know precious little about each other. Although I believe I have an advantage. Braedyn shared much about your family life, but you know little about mine."

"Yet Brae never spoke of me personally?"

"There's one thing I recollect. He mentioned a brother with the temper of a dragon." She giggled and Michael's beaming face lightened the room like a burst of sunlight on a summer's day.

Chapter Thirty-nine

Clare brushed her hair with a long stroke. As a child, the black curls had been the bane of her existence when her mother tried to train its unmanageable ways, and she'd fought the urge to cry over every difficult knot needing to be untangled. How unfortunate her son would deal with the same problem someday.

She gazed at the picture of her parents sitting on the vanity beside her combs. How was it possible she was now a mother herself? When had the years slipped away?

Clare smiled at the photo and continued to brush. As she'd grown older, she had come to appreciate her thick tresses. Many times, after she'd bathed, all she had to do was twist and tie it at the nape of her neck, allow a few tendrils to fall alongside her temples and the look would be complete. Friends remarked how blessed she was that with little fuss her hair held easily and still appeared so lovely.

Rap. Rap.

"Come in."

"You look radiant." Grace admired Clare's reflection in the mirror.

"Why thank you, dear one." She placed the brush aside and turned on the seat. "What can I do for you?"

"I came in to say goodnight and to thank you for such an enjoyable evening with Michael. Dinner was divine. Then the card game afterwards was a pleasurable way to pass the time before he had to leave. It went by too quickly, though." Grace looked heavenward and hugged one of the spindles on the four-poster bed, as if clinging to Michael.

"You look rather radiant yourself. I do believe you're in love."

Grace plopped on the bed and fell backwards, her arms outstretched above her head, golden hair arced around her like angel wings. "Love is divine, is it not?"

"Yes. It's marvelous when the perfect person comes into your life."

Grace sat up and leaned on her elbows. "It appears Michael's ready to be married."

"Really?" Clare rushed to Grace's side and hugged her. "Did he propose?"

They sat side-by-side on the edge of the bed and clasped hands.

"Not exactly, but he said he hoped our

courting days wouldn't last too long because he was ready to be together.

"Wonderful."

"I feel as though I've much to learn before becoming a wife though," Grace said.

"You can be married for years and still feel as if you've not learned a thing."

"Will you teach me? Please?"

Clare released Grace's hand. "I wouldn't know where to begin. You can acquire knowledge from watching my mistakes if that's what you mean." She giggled. "Seriously, though, marriage is a big step and one you can never undo."

"Why would anyone want to be unwed after they've fallen in love? I can't imagine."

"Oh, my, you do have much to discover. But this is not the time to discuss what can go wrong. Right now, enjoy the pleasure of his company and the words of admiration poured over you."

"I shall." Grace shifted sideways and studied Clare.

"Is there something else you wish to discuss? You've become pensive all of a sudden."

"I'd like to share something with you I couldn't speak about earlier during the meal. But I'm not sure how you'll take what I wish to say."

"What is it?"

"It's just —"

"Please speak your mind. You have the freedom to tell me anything."

"It seems Abigail was rather forward today with Michael."

Clare rose, sat in front of the vanity and picked up her brush. "Abigail? Again? Why is it everyone in this house has something against the girl? I'm the only one who seems to defend her."

"Maybe it's because you're unwilling to examine her faults."

"Or no one appreciates her gifts as I do." She dragged the hairbrush roughly through another lock. This time the hair became tangled.

Grace spoke to Clare's reflection. "I know you want to rescue this girl. It's as if you've closed your ears to any counsel regarding her, and you toss away negative comments as if they're a nuisance and not reality."

She slammed the brush down. "Has Christian love and forbearance vanished from this home? Whatever happened to turning the other cheek?"

"You haven't even listened to what I have to say regarding her behavior." Grace touched her shoulder, and Clare felt her anger subside as if cool water had trickled over a flame.

"Does it matter?" She observed Grace in the mirror. "Whatever you say will be intended to turn my heart against another who needs me."

"Then I won't say another word. You're

very dear to me, but I'm afraid the maid has cast a spell over you."

Clare rose and turned towards Grace. "Are you implying I don't have a mind of my own?"

"No. I'm saying you have too big of a heart." Grace kissed Clare's cheek. "One of the many things I love about you. I only hope you don't get hurt."

"Friendships and marriage have a lot in common. We must offer forgiveness and be willing to forget another's faults. What good is caring for someone unless we're willing to defend them when others attack?"

"You're right when you said I have much to learn. I guess the first thing is to not speak my mind."

"That's not what I meant."

"Let's not quarrel over this silly matter. As long as we can share in my joy, what good does it do to disagree?"

Clare stood. "Do you understand why I feel the way I do?"

"I can't say I do. Abigail has acted inappropriately. She needs to be taught what's acceptable and what isn't."

"As we need to be taught how to love another the way Jesus loves us."

"It's a lifetime, is it not?"

"Like marriage." Clare hugged Grace. "Thank you for coming to say goodnight."

Grace left and Clare went back to the vanity. "Dearest Mother, how I wish I could speak with you again. You had such wisdom. No one understands, but I know you would."

She rose, pulled back the bedcovers, blew out the candle on the bedside table and snuggled beneath the eiderdown. Tomorrow would be a new day and the others would have a better outlook on Abigail.

She would do everything in her power to convince them she was right and the girl was worthy of defense. Clare rolled over and hoped sleep would not be as seemingly unachievable as reasoning with her family. Why couldn't they understand Abigail needed their love and support?

She stared towards the ceiling in the dark searching for the answer until her eyes drifted closed.

Chapter Forty

Fredrick set his coffee cup down and leafed through the morning newspaper. "This edition of the *Illustrated London News* surpasses any I've seen until now. Its cover article about the Archbishop of Canterbury, John Bird Sumner, is quite extensive. Did you know Sumner's originally from Kenilworth and received his education at Eton? What did we do before we had this form of information?" He flipped to another page.

James lowered the *Times*. "I'm beginning to appreciate the *London News's* engravings in lieu of the endless advertisement offered in here." He closed the paper and sipped coffee. "I'm grateful George Owen had the foresight to teach the orphans to read. I don't know where I'd be today without his guidance."

Fredrick placed his paper on the edge of

the table. "George is indeed a man before his time. To think he wants every child who comes under his care to have at least an elementary education is superb."

"The Bible was what we were instructed to read. What better material to know and understand than the written Word of God?"

"We must schedule another visit to Alpheton House. I'm sure Margaret and George would enjoy seeing you again."

"And they greatly appreciate the supplies you send twice a year. What did they do before your generosity?"

"They relied on God."

"They still do, I'm sure. There were many nights we wondered where our next meal would come from. George would pray and shortly thereafter there'd be a knock on the door. Either the local baker or someone else would offer enough for all the children to be fed. Miracle after miracle happened."

"Like Jesus with the fishes and loaves."

"Exactly. But I was too young at the time to appreciate how many prayers were answered every day."

Clare entered rubbing her eyes. "Good morning, Father. James." Although she was clothed and apparently ready for the day her steps were slow and responses systematic. She slumped in a chair next to James.

"You seemed to have had a rough night's

sleep."

"I must admit it was rather restless."

"I'm sorry. Is something bothering you?" James gestured towards the manservant who poured Clare a cup of coffee and offered her a serviette.

Clare yawned and shrugged.

"What is it?" Fredrick asked.

"May I be honest?"

"I expect nothing less."

"I can't get over how everyone seems to have something against Abigail." She raised a palm towards them. "I know. I know. You two don't appreciate her either. You don't have to tell me again."

"What's she done now?"

"I don't know." Clare sat upright, draped the serviette across her lap and added a sugar cube to the drink. "Supposedly there was an incident with Michael yesterday. I didn't pursue the details."

"What will it take for you to see she's not what you'd hoped?" James asked.

"Do either of you know anything about her? How she was tossed aside as an infant and abused in foster care? James, you of all people should have a heart for someone with her background."

"Is that what she's told you?" James patted the top of her hand.

"Yes, and I believe her." She pulled away.

"I saw a scar along her arm. She's a wounded soul who needs tender loving care. Would God have us treat her otherwise?"

"When you were a child, you wanted to bring home every stray animal you found," Fredrick said tenderly. "I'm not surprised you have a heart for her, too."

"You're the one who taught me to care for others. Like you did with James. Weren't you the one who convinced me James needed our attention?"

"Yes." Fredrick winked at his son-in-law. "And he's proved worthy of the investment, has he not?"

She reached for James's hand, intertwining her fingers with his. "Absolutely. Then how's Abigail any different?"

"All I'm trying to say is there are some people who are shrewd. When I met James I knew he was a man of character."

"We've had this conversation over and over. I always feel as if I'm the only one willing to give Abigail the benefit of the doubt."

"If you say so, Clare. But could it be you aren't giving the rest of us the benefit of *your* doubt?"

"Would you pass the paper, please?" She flipped open the newspaper. "On second thought, I'll take this to the parlor."

"Aren't you going to eat something?" He pointed to the buffet of options the staff had prepared.

"I'm not really hungry." Clare rose and gathered her drink. "Maybe I'll feel more like eating later on."

The door closed with a silent click.

James's eyebrows rose. "Are you going to say anything to her?"

"Not yet. Clare would merely get defensive again."

"But shouldn't she know?"

"What can we tell her? There needs to be collaboration before we can make any unverified accusations."

"I don't like keeping things from Clare."

"Nor do I, but until we have solid evidence, we can't say anything."

"If you're certain."

"What you showed me must be proven. Until then, we mustn't say a word. Agree?"

"Agree."

James lifted the *London News*.

Fredrick sipped his coffee and caught his reflection in the large windowpane. In the ripple of the glass, his dear Florence's face appeared. She had always encouraged him to speak the truth in love, and insisted they raise Clare with the same motto. After Florence's death, he continued to teach his daughter the importance of honesty, yet at the same time he wanted to protect her from any form of harm. How could he expose the facts to Clare without breaking her heart? Was he truly trying to be her protector or was he in fact a coward?

The Lord would have to reveal to him how to share the lies and secrets being told in his home.

Lord, give me your wisdom and guidance. You know my heart and my daughter's spirit. I pray she'll trust me as I trust You. Amen.

Chapter Forty-one

Clare curled into the corner of the settee, draped a blanket over her legs to ward off the morning rawness and sipped her hot drink.

Frost edged the outside windows. Sunlight filtered through the doily-type designs and produced a work of resplendent crystals, a mesmerizing masterpiece intricately drawn by the Creator's fingertips.

Clare put the cup down and drew the blanket closer.

Even the beautiful patterns were a short-lived distractor.

What would it take to convince Father and James of Abigail's worth? Nothing short of a supernatural intervention. Was it possible the two men she admired most were blinded by their gender? Somehow women were beneath them and could be discarded with the flick of a wrist? Clare shook her head. Never. They might be stubborn at times, but she'd never known either man to be narrow-minded.

Clare bolted upright.

Wait a minute. What about a party?

She'd make it a grand affair. Allow Abigail to demonstrate how efficient she was. With Clare's help, Abigail could show the household she was capable of handling challenging deeds. Afterwards, James and Father would have to acquiesce. The negative bantering had become tiresome and might finally end. She was ready for a decision to be made about Jean's replacement. It would be the first step for the family to move on in their grief and get the house back in order.

She mentally prepared a list of food, music and attendees. They'd invite the Tripps, Phoebe's parents, Michael, and others in their social circle.

Grace and Elizabeth drifted into the room. "May we join you?"

"Certainly." She clapped with excitement and the blanket slipped off her lap. "I can't wait to tell you about an extravagant idea I've had."

"What is it?" Elizabeth lifted the covering from the floor, put it back in place and sat. Grace perched on the harpsichord bench.

"Why don't we have a festive gathering? Everyone needs some merriment to stave off the doldrums. Why not share in some fun here at Bethel?"

Grace leapt lightly from the bench. "What a wonderful idea. I do hope Michael can come."

"There's no doubt, he'll do everything in his power. He'd use any excuse to see you again." Clare pulled a pad and pencil from a nearby drawer.

"Have you spoken to Fredrick about this?" Elizabeth asked. "He's definitely feeling better, however we mustn't put any extra strain on him now he's improved."

"The beauty is, we can put this together without him. With James and Sam's help, Father needn't worry about anything. What do you say?"

"I say it's wonderful." Grace did a pirouette. "I love balls. We can wear our finest gowns and dance like kings and queens all night long."

"We'll have the furniture rearranged to make room for dancing."

Clare jotted down each suggestion. "To begin, we need to decide when to have the party."

"The sooner the better, don't you think?" Grace stopped mid-skip.

"It'll take some time to order the food and send out invitations," Elizabeth said.

"If we begin right now, we might be able to have it in a fortnight." Clare penciled the date.

"Seems a manageable timeframe."

"It's settled." She put aside the paper and

pencil.

"How very exciting. And to think I expected to be bored today after such a lovely evening last night." Grace's eyes sparkled like the doily designs on the windows.

"Before we make any arrangements, I suggest we present this to Fredrick and James. After all, they need to make the final decision." Elizabeth stood. "I don't want to put a damper on our excitement. I think it's a marvelous idea, but we need to consider everyone else."

"I suppose we should. It's good to have someone with some sense." Clare rose and hugged Elizabeth. "I'm grateful for you."

Elizabeth tilted her head. "Clare, is the true reason for this event to help others with the doldrums?"

"A portion of it."

"The other reason?"

Clare placed hands on hips and compressed her lips. "To show Father what Abigail is capable of doing."

"There's no need to become upset. We all want what's best for our home. Don't we?"

"I suppose." Clare released her hands.

"Let's work together to make this the best party ever held in Bethel Manor."

"First, we must talk to Father." Clare folded the blanket, lifted her cup and headed to the dining room. Elizabeth and Grace followed.

"What's this?" Father lifted his head from

the news. "The three of you look as if you're scheming together about something."

"Where'd James go?" Clare scanned the room. "We wanted to speak to both of you about a wonderful idea we know you'll agree to."

"Hold on. When you start off with a statement like that you make me want to consider whether I'll truly think it's wonderful." Her father smirked. "Go on. What is it?"

"What do you think about a party?"

Her father straightened. Frowned. Turned away slightly and gazed out the window. He tapped the tabletop and hummed under his breath. Finally, he looked at them and smiled. "I think it's the best idea I've heard in quite some time."

Clare jumped in place and clapped. "I knew it."

"We'll hire out new staff and bring in someone to play—"

"Wait a minute."

"What's the matter?"

"Why hire new staff when we have a perfectly capable retinue right here?"

"They're ready for a break, Clare. Most are too tired to do their daily chores, never mind adding something extra for our benefit. Surely you understand my reasons?"

"I understand no such thing. You're making this suggestion so Abigail won't partake."

"She didn't even cross my mind. Since you mention it, I do believe it's beyond her capabilities."

Clare spun around, walked out the door and slammed it behind her.

Chapter Forty-two

Rap. Rap.

"Go away."

"I'm not going anywhere." Clare's father spoke from outside the closed bedroom door. "You didn't get your stubbornness from your mother. You got it from me, and I'll stand out here as long as necessary."

She flung open the door.

Father leaned casually against the frame with his arms crossed. "May I come in please?"

She stepped aside and allowed him access. "How can you be so close-minded?"

He took her arms and held them firmly. "Look me in the eye, young lady. Have you ever known me to be anything but fair to others? If so, can you please enlighten me when that might've been?"

She lowered her eyes and shook her head.

"Do you think for one minute I enjoy not

believing in someone under my own roof?"

She slipped out from his clasp. "No."

"Clare, I don't remember a time when you didn't trust me. When did I lose your confidence?"

"This has nothing to do with whether I trust you or not."

"What does it have to do with? Are you behaving this way because you want to give Abigail a fair chance, or because you want your own way regardless of the outcome?"

"That's unfair."

"Is it?"

"What do you possibly have against this girl?" She sat on the vanity chair and faced him.

"If I try and explain, are you willing to listen? It seems Grace tried to say something to you last night and you wouldn't hear her story either."

"Oh, now everyone's talking about me behind my back." How dare they come together like a flock of nattering hens and conspire against her?

"We've done no such thing. What we want is to figure out what's going on and keep this family intact in the process. Don't you see how Abigail's manipulated you?"

"No, I don't."

"This story of her upbringing? Have you verified what she's told you?"

"Since when do we question someone

else's life story?"

"May I ask you something?" He sat across from her and placed his hands on his knees. The creases across his brow deepened. A pained expression lodged in his eyes and spread into the fine lines alongside them. "You know I love you, don't you?"

"Of course, Father. Without question, I do." A lump in her throat grew as he gazed at her with tenderness intertwined with the pain. She had never intended to hurt this man who had always been her rock.

"And I would never do anything to cause you distress."

She examined her nails and her fingers blurred. "I know that as well."

"What would it take for us to compromise? Would you be willing to let me hire others and let Abigail work beside them?"

Clare adjusted her dress and pressed creases from her lap. "But how will you know what she's capable of if you don't give her greater tasks."

"I want to see firsthand she's willing to do whatever it takes to show me she's open to advice and able to work on a team. You want to put her in a position of authority, but even Jesus said we are to serve and not be served. Do you think she's able to serve without having authority?"

"She's perfectly capable of doing

whatever's asked of her."

"This way I can let our own staff have the night off, and they can go and be with their families." Her father leaned forward, his hands still pressed into his knees. "Let's never let these little matters tear at our relationship, my precious one."

"Thank you for giving me this opportunity to demonstrate Abigail's worth."

"It's not up to you, my dear girl, to prove another's worth." He reached out, helped her up and stood eye-to-eye. "But I admire how diligent you've been in defending her, no matter what. You're a good friend. I hope she recognizes your firm support."

Clare pecked his cheek. "Any compassion I have, I learned from you. As well as my stubbornness." She hugged him longer than usual, unwilling to be released from his strong arms and reassure him of her love.

Her father's eyes floated in a sea of love. "You are just like your mother."

"And she would say I'm like you."

"True."

He put his hand on the small of her back as they made their way into the hallway. "I'm grateful we had this talk, Father. I'll be down shortly and start writing out invitations. First I must go and to speak with Abigail."

"Do you want me to break the news to her? I've nothing to lose. She's already upset with me."

"We have a good relationship. I'll ask for her assistance in ordering the food, if you agree, to soften the blow she won't be in charge."

"A splendid idea."

Her father left along the center staircase to his office while Clare made her way to the kitchen.

Approaching the kitchen entrance, she stopped and listened. The harshness in Abigail's voice was unmistakable, but who could she be speaking to in such a tone?

"You idiot." Abigail growled. "How dare you say anything about me to the Master? I'll have your neck in a noose."

"I didn't say nothing." Everett's deep voice seemed to scratch with tension.

"You better not 've. And if I ever find out you did —"

"What's going on here?" Clare stepped into the warm room.

"Nothing, miss." Abigail scooted backwards as if she'd seen a large rodent. "We were just talking."

"It sounded as if you were threatening him." She gestured towards Everett.

"I'd never do such a thing, ma'am." Abigail sniveled. "Beg your pardon, ma'am, but I'm sure you misunderstood. Didn't she, Everett?"

Her father's manservant gave a nod.

Clare eyed Abigail. Was she playacting or was it fear in the maid's eyes? She could have sworn Abigail had been shouting when she'd first arrived.

"Are you certain nothing untoward is going on, Everett?"

"Yes, miss."

"Very well. Abigail, could I speak with you privately?"

Abigail curtsied. "Yes, miss. Whatever you need. Everett, would you please finish the chore you were assigned? I greatly appreciate your hard work on the family's behalf." The girl smiled coyly, almost teasingly in the manservant's direction.

Had she missed something between these two? One minute they were fighting, and the next he acted as if Abigail were the best thing since an apple tart.

Chapter Forty-three

Clare gathered her writing pens and entered the sitting room to use the pearl-inlaid desk belonging to her mother. Beside the fire, Grace sat slumped in a chair, her eyes scrunched closed.

Oh, dear!" She rushed to Grace's side. "What's wrong?"

"Yes, I believe so." Grace opened her eyes. Her pupils were dilated and she appeared confused.

Clare squatted beside the chair to touch Grace's head. "There doesn't seem to be a fever, but you look dreadful. May I get anything for you?"

"I need to rest a few minutes. I'll be fine."

"You seemed cheerful only a short while ago. What's happened since we spoke about the party and you were twirling around this room?"

"Nothing. I've only had a cup of tea. Then

I felt dizzy, sat for a moment and you entered." Grace tried to get up and leaned on the arm of the chair. "I may need to retire to my room."

"Let me help you." Clare guided her by the arm up the stairs into her private chamber.

"I was looking forward to assisting with penning the invitations. I hope I can help a bit later."

"If you feel up to it. You need to rest for now."

Grace lay across the bed with her forearm resting across her eyes.

"Shall I send for Doctor Willard?"

"That's not necessary."

"I'll check on you in an hour. If you aren't any better, I'll insist he come."

"Thank you, Clare. I just need a few minutes' rest and I'll be fine." Grace rolled over on her side.

Clare draped a cream-colored coverlet over her and tiptoed out.

James waited at the bottom of the center staircase. "Is everything all right? I saw you helping Grace to her room."

"I'm afraid she's been overcome with a spell of dizziness."

James headed up the stairs. She placed a hand on his. "I promised her I'd check in a little while to see how she's doing. Right now, she's resting."

"Should the doctor come?"

"Let's see how she does. I won't hesitate to send for him if she hasn't improved."

"Thank you."

"May we chat for a few minutes?" she asked.

"Certainly."

Clare held James's hand as they made their way to the parlor.

"What is it?" James released her fingers as they sat together on the settee.

"I need your advice."

Her husband's mouth curled into a darling, boyish smile. "Well, well. That's not what I expected to hear."

"What did you imagine I'd say?"

"Perhaps a reprimand for something I may've done without realizing it. You know, like husbands tend to do." His thin face lit up. When they'd first met, she'd thought him gangly with sallow cheeks. When Jean fattened him up a bit, his features took on a healthy glow. Now she couldn't look at him without becoming disarmed. His beautiful eyes seemed to bore into her soul and read her every thought.

"Stop looking at me like that," she teased.

"Like what? As if I adore you? What's wrong with a husband who thinks his wife is breathtaking?"

She shrugged. "Nothing. Every woman dreams of a man who'll gaze at her with adoration. Yet you make me blush like a new bride when I see the passion in your eyes."

He scooted closer and whispered. "When I see you, the fervor burns within."

Clare moved nearer. "This isn't why I asked to speak with you."

"I gathered not." He kissed her with the youthful desire of their early years of marriage.

After a minute, she backed away, placing a palm over the base of her throat. "You take my breath away."

"We're even. You took my heart five years ago. Last year you gave me our precious George."

Clare lowered her eyes. "You're such a dear putting up with me."

James sat back and reached for her hand. "Tell me what's on your mind."

"I've forgotten what I wished to say now you've distracted me."

He chuckled. "I'm not sure what I find more amusing. Not being reprimanded when I expected to be, or my ability to divert your thoughts entirely and so easily."

She tapped his arm gently. "I owe you an apology and need your advice."

"I'm not sure why you feel a need to apologize."

"I've been defensive, hardheaded about Abigail."

"Ah. What's made you realize there may be a problem with her?"

"Father and I had a long chat. He started me thinking about my perspective of the girl after I overheard her in the kitchen. She spoke quite sharply to Everett who's such a dear man he wouldn't hurt a fly. I felt as if she were taking advantage of his nature."

"Apology accepted, but it's one of the many things I admire about you. You don't back down. Especially when it comes to someone you're advocating for. What advice do you seek?"

"I realize we all have angry moments. It could have been a one-off response on her part. More than anything, I want to give Abigail the benefit of the doubt."

"It's only natural." James rose, stoked the fire with the large billows and sat back down. "What's the problem?"

"Can everyone I love be wrong about Abigail? Or am I'm being blind in my zeal to defend her?"

"No one is ever as they appear, Clare. We try to mask our true identity in order to be accepted. When you think about it, we only let ourselves be known when we sense a freedom of acceptance."

"And I want her to know I accept her when no one else does."

"On the other hand…"

"Yes?"

"We can be deceived by someone who

uses a ruse. Wolves dressed in sheep clothing."

"How do you know the difference?"

"Be wise."

"And?"

"Don't be fooled. You're no simpleton, Clare. Be alert to what's going on. Listen to what your heart tells you." James touched her lips with his fingertip.

"My heart tells me I love you."

"And I you."

"I'm going to be more attentive to Abigail. This upcoming party might reveal who she truly is."

Chapter Forty-four

Clare waited at the end of Grace's bed. A sickly sweet odor, redolent of when Father had been ill, floated over the room. If it weren't cold outside, she'd be tempted to open a sash to clear the air. "What do you think?"

"How very odd." Doctor Willard lifted Grace's eyelids one by one. "She's demonstrating the same symptoms as when Fredrick fell ill."

"Do you have any idea what it can be?" James held his sister's hand. His wayward curl dropped forward into the deep crease formed between his brows. He studied the doctor as he checked her pulse. "She looks fragile."

"I'm going to discuss with the apothecary to see if he can offer some advice."

"How does that help?"

"There's got to be a reason why two members of this household have suffered the same thing. I've not seen this in any of my other patients, otherwise I'd be concerned about the beginnings of an epidemic. The rest of you must be alert to what you eat and drink."

"Grace mentioned having tea prior to becoming unwell," Clare said.

"I can't imagine this has come from tea, but I'll bear that in mind."

"What can we do for her?"

"Allow plenty of rest. I'll leave some herbal mix for Grace to consume every few hours to keep her from becoming dehydrated. They seemed to help Fredrick in his recovery."

"What's going on here?" Clare's father and Elizabeth crossed the threshold.

"It seems Grace has come down with what you suffered from, Father." Clare stepped up to them.

"She'll be fine, son." Her father squeezed James's shoulder. "Doctor Willard knows what's best. He took great care of me."

"She was looking forward to the party," Clare said.

"And Grace will still be able to enjoy it." Elizabeth's concerned frown contradicted the intended encouraging words.

"Yes, she will." Father offered a nod. "I'm proof she'll recover."

"In the meantime, I insist everyone leave and let her sleep." The doctor closed his satchel and led the group of onlookers out.

James hesitated by the door. "Perhaps I can stay and we can take shifts?"

"There's no need. She'll rest fine now. I'll return in a few hours after I've visited Mister Barnsley at Sunflower Cottage. He suffers dreadfully from gout. Aging isn't mankind's friend."

"Thank you for always being available when we need you most." Fredrick shook his hand.

"After I've checked in on Grace again, I'll visit Sam. I haven't seen him since Jean's passing and the small gathering you had at the house."

"I'm sure he'd appreciate you calling in."

Clare leaned back against the bannister. "I was preparing the invitations, but I must admit my enthusiasm has waned since I found Grace."

"Why don't we take a stroll around the gardens. We'd all feel better," James said.

"Do you think we should send word to Michael? He'll want to know."

"Why worry the man?"

"I think he should be made aware. What if he gets news via the servants who talk to each other from house to house? You know how news rapidly spreads."

"Perhaps that's a good idea."

"I'll send him a quick note."

"After you finish we'll go for a walk." James brushed his curl back revealing the deep crease still etched in his forehead. "I need some fresh air."

"We'll meet you in the foyer in a few minutes." Fredrick and Elizabeth headed down the stairs.

+ + +

"It's amazing how twenty minutes outside can clear your mind. I feel revived." James and Clare waited at the front of Bethel for Elizabeth and Fredrick to catch up.

"As do I." Clare handed her cloak to Everett as the four entered the house.

James removed his hat but retained his coat. "I'm going back out to the stables and check on the workers. Encourage them. That sort of thing."

"I'm ready to begin again on the invitations. I'm determined this party will go ahead as planned."

"There's no reason not to. Grace shall be dancing the night away in a fortnight."

Fredrick took off his outerwear and handed them to the manservant. "Most assuredly. Once I took a few doses of the doctor's medicinal herbs, it was a matter of days and I was up and about. Although I must say, it was a bit disconcerting how confused I felt for those few days."

Clare released a low exhale. "I'm grateful you've completely recovered."

"As am I. Now I've some work to attend to. James was able to handle most of the bills, but I've a few personal notes I need to send."

"Shall I help you with the invitations, Clare?" Elizabeth offered.

"That would be lovely. I just need to go to my room and get my personal seal and wax."

"I'll wait for you in the parlor."

+ + +

"Now where did I leave those things?" Clare rummaged around her vanity, peered under the bed and bedside chair. She recalled leaving them on the corner side table but they weren't there either.

She headed back downstairs.

Abigail carried a tray in her direction.

"Where are you delivering this?" Clare asked.

"To Miss Grace's room."

"Did anyone ring you?"

"Why no, miss, I thought it would be fine to offer her something warm to drink since she's unwell."

"The doctor says she's to remain undisturbed."

Abigail curtsied. "Yes, ma'am. Everett mentioned you just returned from a walk. Shall I bring a fresh pot of tea to the parlor?"

"It's very kind of you to ask. But I think Miss Elizabeth and myself are fine for the moment."

"Perhaps later."

Abigail turned to leave.

"By the way…"

The maid glanced over her shoulder. "Yes, miss?"

"By any chance, have you seen my seal set? I've seemed to have misplaced it."

"No. I don't believe I have. But I'm very happy to see if I can find it."

"Thank you. I'd appreciate it."

"It's my pleasure to do anything I can to serve you, miss. You've done more than any girl could ask for." Abigail turned and continued toward the kitchen.

"That maid is complex." Clare said to Elizabeth as she entered the parlor.

"To whom are you referring?" Elizabeth waited near the desk. Her rosy cheeks and sparkling expression made her appearance angelic. It was no wonder Father had the demeanor of an infatuated schoolboy whenever she was in his presence.

"Abigail."

"Ah. What has she done now?"

"Earlier, I overheard her reprimanding Everett. When I confronted her, she was deeply remorseful. Now she's demonstrating selflessness in serving Grace and me."

"We both know women are the most difficult species God ever created to comprehend." Elizabeth's eyes twinkled as she scooped her skirt under her and sat at the desk.

"Indeed, we are." Clare handed her a

blank invitation.

Chapter Forty-five

Clare opened the door. "You wasted no time, Michael."

"As soon as I received your note, I came straight away after making a quick stop at Thomas's." Michael leaned over to catch his breath.

"The doctor says she'll be fine. I just didn't want you to hear secondhand."

"May I see her?"

"I'm sorry. It's not permissible and could appear indiscreet."

"Where's James? There's another reason I've come."

"He's at the stable yard with Sam."

"I'll go find him." He tapped his cap and dashed down the path.

+ + +

"Who's running like mad in this

direction?" James gestured towards a looming figure.

Sam started moving in the man's direction. "We need to be watchful of villains that've been stealing fowl from the pens."

James walked alongside him tightly gripping a stick, the two ready to apprehend any trespasser by the collar and send them reeling back down the lane.

Sam skidded to a halt. "What're we thinking? Master Fredrick would be upset with us if we didn't offer this stranger a drink and food. It's his way."

"You're right." He released his tight grip. "I should never forget his generosity to me. It changed my life. The other thing I'll never fail to recall was Jean's jolly chatter whenever I sat at the kitchen table and watched her work."

"She was a bright morning star." Sam semi-smiled. "I'm grateful you've memories of my lass. I still miss her, but thankful I've got the Shaws. Been my family since I was a lad."

"I say, he's no stranger." James and Sam caught up with the breathless Michael. "What are you doing here?"

"Came…as…soon…"

"Give yourself a minute, lad," Sam said. "Don't want you faintin' on us."

Michael took several deep breaths.

"I wasn't sure Clare should have sent the note. I figured you'd rush here to see her. I'm appreciative you cared enough to come this rapidly, though," James said.

Michael took off his cap and examined his feet as if he were about to take off. "Um."

"What is it? You look like you're about to be quite ill. Perhaps the doctor needs to see you as well when he returns." James ribbed Sam and winked.

"I was wondering…"

"Yes?"

"I was wondering if…"

"Spit it out, son." Sam feigned impatience as he gave James a soft, conspiratorial kick. "We've not got all day. The horses need their feed and stalls mucked."

Michael looked up. "Since your father's no longer living, James, I thought it only proper to ask you."

"I'm not sure what my father has to do with anything." James covered his mouth with a closed fist to stifle a chuckle. This poor man was about to faint yet he couldn't help but toy with his emotions. He remembered sweating profusely when he's asked Fredrick's permission to marry Clare. Michael was demonstrating the same discomfort and James enjoyed watching him perspire in the crisp air.

"I'd like to marry your sister, Grace."

"Why didn't you say so in the first place?" James clapped him on the back. "Of course you have my consent. I can't think of another man I'd rather have as part of the family. Does she expect this?"

"We talked briefly about it when we were together last. When I heard she was unwell, I realized how much I cared for her. She's a jewel Braedyn found for me. I could never replace him, but I will love Grace as deeply as he did."

"Let's go back to the house and break the news to Fredrick and Mother. They'll be extremely happy. We despaired over the loss of Brae, and Grace's heart was broken." James draped an arm over Sam. "Join us. The horses can wait a few more minutes. You're a member of the family. You should be a part of this joyous occasion."

Sam's grin spread across his face. "Thank you, Master James. I'd like that very much. There's been too much sadness in Bethel's walls. It's time she's filled with joy again. My Jean would want everyone to move on with their lives."

+ + +

"Here they come. Move away from the window." Clare indicated to Elizabeth. The two sat in respective chairs, picked up sewing and pretended to stitch.

James, Sam and Michael passed the parlor window, and the front door opened and closed.

If each man had swallowed the noonday sun there wouldn't be as much light as they showed with facial joy when they entered the room.

Clare stopped her pretense of stitching. "What are you three doing here? I thought you were busy at the stables?"

"Where's your father?" James asked.

"I believe he's in the office." Elizabeth pulled at a pretend thread.

"Sam, why don't you and Michael wait here while I go for him?"

"I can ring for Abigail, and she can tell Father's he's wanted."

"Sending for her is probably not a good idea."

She shrugged. "I suppose it's not."

"I'll be back momentarily with him." James left.

Michael marched back and forth in front of the fireplace while Sam positioned himself just inside the room.

"Are you all right, Michael?" Elizabeth put her sewing aside. "I do hope you aren't worried about Grace. I'm sure she'll be fine."

"In fact, we're convinced enough she will quickly recover, we're going to have a party." Clare went to the desk and retrieved several invitations. "Could you please deliver these to Simeon and Thomas? Here's one for you as well."

Michael took the cards and stowed them in his coat pocket, his hand shaking.

Clare's father entered with James. "I

understand you wish to share something with us, young man."

Michael's mustache twitched and he looked upward. "Um. Yes, sir. If I may, sir?"

"Mother." James sat beside Elizabeth. "Michael has something he'd like to say."

"To me?" She held a handkerchief near her eyes and dabbed gently.

"Ma'am. I would like yours and Mister Shaw's permission to marry Grace. I've already asked James and he's kindly agreed."

Chapter Forty-six

Clare's eyelids fluttered. She blinked. A white light, otherworldly in resplendence, bathed the bedroom.

She grabbed a shawl and made her way to the window. The full moon's glow seemed powerful enough to shatter the pane. She pressed a palm against the wavy glass and its coldness penetrated her skin. God's nighttime illuminations never ceased to amaze — whether the moon hung with a bare thread of presence or shouted in full glory as it was doing right now. Below the window, shadows from bare branches created zigzag patterns on the sleeping garden. Melting snow during daylight hours was frozen in time, a mere dusting of ghostly lumps.

Clare lit a candle. Grace was still unaware of the happiness awaiting her. Her room was only a short distance down the corridor. As long as she was awake, she'd check in on her. Doctor

Willard had stopped by the parlor as Michael made his proclamation and reassured them Grace was doing much better.

Everyone had been caught up in the excitement they'd nearly forgotten Grace had been ill, but the doctor's assessment had been an encouragement and they retired for the night with renewed hope. Michael had remained in anticipation of seeing Grace revived enough in the morning to ask for her hand in marriage.

The candle cast its own shadows along the dark paneled walls. She was familiar with each nook and cranny in the house and managed to find her way around even when her eyes had been blinded by illness. The candle was merely keeping her company but would come in handy when she reached Grace. Even though the moonlight would be sufficient, she didn't want to take the chance and disturb her unnecessarily.

Sour aroma's of sickness permeating the space earlier had dissipated and was replaced with perfumed herbs used for Grace's consumption. The doctor had also made a mixture of dried spices and petals, wrapped in several cloths and placed them around the area. The combination made the surroundings serene.

Clare drew close to Grace. She slept peacefully, her breathing calm. A sleeping princess. Michael would be blessed beyond measure to have this woman as his betrothed.

She tiptoed out, headed back through the

hall and hesitated. Perhaps a warm drink would help in getting back to sleep. Clare made her way down the back stairs and into the kitchen.

She paused. Abigail's back faced her. What was the girl doing up at this time of night? Was she that conscientious she worked well into the wee hours to make up for the others inabilities? Abigail had moaned about the servants not keeping up with their duties.

"Ahem."

Abigail jumped.

"I'm sorry. I tried not to startle you, but surely you should be in bed by now."

Abigail turned her back to Clare and seemed to gather into a pile whatever she had been tending to. "I couldn't sleep, miss."

"Nor I. There's so much excitement going on at present. I'm sure everyone's heard Michael wishes to marry Grace."

"Yes, miss, we've heard. I do hope this works out for the best." Abigail draped her stack with a tea towel.

"What can you possible mean?" Clare covered her mouth and yawned.

"It's just there's gossip. But no one believes it."

"What kind of rumors and about whom?"

"Mister Michael. He's well known in Ely. Let's just say...he's...known about town by every woman living there. But I mustn't pass on rumors. I'm sorry, miss."

Clare sat at the large table where Jean had listened to her moan about her father, cry over James, grunt about this and that while keeping opinions to herself. The place would never be the same without her dear friend and mentor no matter how much she dreamed to have it returned to those days.

She desperately wanted to give Abigail a chance, yet there was no denying she didn't know when to keep quiet. She had something negative to say about everyone. What else was Clare missing in the maid's character?

"What were you doing when I came in?" Clare pushed away from the table and went to the counter where Abigail seemed to be standing guard.

"Um. Nothing, miss."

"What are you trying to hide? I insist you tell me." Clare glanced around the maid but the towel covered the evidence.

"If you must know, it's…a…surprise."

"For whom?"

Abigail reached under the towel and pulled out Clare's seal and wax. "One is for you, miss."

She squealed. "How wonderful. I can finish the invitations now. Where in the world did you find them?"

"In your room, miss. I was going to give them to you first thing in the morning."

There was no way the seal had been

where Abigail claimed. Clare had personally checked every imaginable place. But why would the maid lie? "That's very kind."

"May I go to bed now, miss? Once I put these other things away?" Abigail covered her mouth as if stifling a yawn.

"Certainly. I think I shall retire too. Thank you again for finding these things."

"You're welcome, miss. I would do anything to help you." Abigail curtsied and waited, still guarding the covered items.

"Well, goodnight."

"Goodnight, miss."

Clare closed the door and circled around to the other side of the kitchen where she could observe Abigail unnoticed.

With conspiratorial glances, the maid scanned the kitchen. She lifted the towel. Underneath was a tray. The bluebell teapot and cups were arranged as if prepared for guests. Abigail lifted the lid of the teapot, stirred and sniffed whatever was brewing.

Why in the world would she hide those things? There was more to her maid than she wanted to admit. Were the others in the house more astute than she, after all? Perhaps tomorrow she would give more thought to her insistence Abigail was the ideal person for the job. Secrecy and lies were not permissible no matter how much she wanted to be right about the girl's potential.

Chapter Forty-seven

James rested the newspaper on the table. Loud chatter in the dining room sounded like summer bees buzzing in the large chestnut trees lining Bethel's drive. The pink and white blossoms drew the worker bees, and their hives thrived with activity. From the insects' hard work, honey eventually made its way to the breakfast table and dripped from delicious toast and crumpets.

In this beehive of activity, a servant girl spooned honeyed syrup into a small container as the clamor around her rose. A stream of fine gold from the spoon caught the sunlight and glinted like a fire opal.

Elizabeth and Clare chattered with growing volume about the upcoming party.

Fredrick directed Everett on the day's events while the servants clattered cutlery and dishes along the serving table.

Abigail brought in a tray and set it down. She proceeded to prepare tea, her demeanor quiet in comparison to the commotion.

The door opened.

James waved Michael into the room. "Good morning. You'll discover this morning how raucous the family can be. Especially when there's reason for a celebration. When you see the chaos, you may change your mind about becoming part of us."

Michael's ruddy mustache lifted with a wide grin. "I won't change my mind. And I don't mind the noise. I grew up with ten siblings. Asking you, Fredrick and Elizabeth for Grace's hand in marriage was what I dreaded most. That was harder than hauling creosote bags in Ely's shipyard for ten hours."

"Have some coffee." Fredrick nodded with a smile to Michael. "I only need a few more minutes with Everett and we'll be finished with business."

Clare's father seemed a different person since recovering from the frightening ordeal with his health. More youthful. Confident. Fredrick had also resumed much of the daily paperwork and running of the estate.

"Staff, in order of rank, will visit their family two days at a time." Fredrick indicated a list of names to his manservant. "Be sure to post this where everyone can check their designated days. If there are any questions refer them to

Sam."

"Yes, sir."

"Sam will be in charge of the rotation and see to it the handoff of tasks will be done efficiently and proceed as usual around the estate."

Everett accepted the paperwork from Fredrick and exited.

Michael sat beside James. "It's an honor to be here with everyone."

"There's no better place to be than at this table." James scanned the room. "It's amazing how God has brought us together from different backgrounds. Why are we surprised when He works such wonders?"

"I certainly don't deserve to be here. I come from a poor crop holder's family in Ireland. They barely manage to find enough food to eat."

"And I come from an orphanage where there never seemed to be enough, yet we survived." James sensed the rawness of his emotions. Of where he'd been as a child and where God had brought him. Many times, he had doubted the reality of God and questioned George and Margaret Owen time and again about the foolishness of their faith. Yet even in James's doubts, God had proven Himself worthy of his trust.

The door creaked. Raucous noises halted. Heads turned towards the entrance.

Grace floated in, her face pale and drawn. Her usually thin features, now even slimmer, made her eyes appear wider, bluer. "What in the world's going on?"

James and Michael jumped from their chairs.

Grace stepped up to Michael. "What are *you* doing here?" The pallid coloring along her cheeks and jaw subtly transformed into a hue of pink. Radiant life returned to her skin.

"He came to see me," James teased.

Grace looked at him with raised eyebrows.

"Please sit." Michael gently guided her to the table and pulled out a chair. "You must still feel weak."

"Did you really come to see James?" she whispered as she sat.

"Yes." Michael's coloring now matched hers. "But it was you that made me seek him out."

"Me?" Grace examined Michael's face and looked up at those who observed as if suddenly conscious she and Michael were being watched.

Michael took her hands and knelt. "I was hoping to ask you privately. But it seems that won't happen."

"What do you wish to say?"

"Will you please...if you would consider..."

"Just ask her, man," James prodded.

"Would you please be my wife?"

Grace withdrew a hand and put it over her mouth. Tears glistened along her cheeks and pooled into the top of her fingers. She nodded.

Clapping erupted. Elizabeth and Clare squealed.

"It seems you already have approval from the rest." She surveyed the spectators with a wide smile.

Michael pulled out a chair and perched on it in front of Grace. "You weren't well enough to ask last night. James and Fredrick kindly offered to let me stay until you had improved. You're much better this morning than I'd hoped."

"You do seem to have improved quickly," Clare said.

"I'm sure it's all due to Doctor Willard."

Abigail set the teapot and cups before Grace and quietly moved away. James noted the side-glance the maid had given Michael. What was the girl thinking? Was it a glimpse of lust or loathing?

Grace slightly pushed the cup aside. "I think I'd better wait a few more days before I have anything to eat or drink except what the doctor has prescribed."

"You wouldn't mind if I have the tea, would you?" Clare came around the table and proceeded to pour herself a drink.

"By all means," Grace said.

"Miss, shall I bring you a fresh pot?" Abigail rushed to Clare's side.

"No, thank you, but that's very kind of you to offer. It hasn't steeped too long. I'm sure it's fine."

Abigail grabbed the cup. Tea sloshed over the tablecloth, down Grace's clothing and onto the floor. Those around the table jumped from the hot drink. "Oh, dear. I'm sorry, miss. I was just trying to help."

"You nearly burned us." Clare scowled. "What were you thinking?"

The maid grabbed a towel and proceeded to wipe up the spill.

"Never mind the mess. Please help Miss Grace clean up."

"As soon as I take the tea away, I will serve her," Abigail said.

"Leave the tea and do as I say." The harshness of Clare's tone made the girl flinch.

Only moments before the room had been overflowing with jubilation. Now it was filled with confusion and anger. Enough was enough. Something had to be done with the wretched girl.

James needed to speak with Clare. He had to let her know what he and Fredrick had uncovered about Abigail.

Chapter Forty-eight

Clare followed her father and James into the office. Why had they insisted she come with them instead of staying in the dining area to supervise Abigail and the necessary cleaning from the spilled tea? Surely this meeting could wait.

The two men she adored most in the world stepped behind the desk as comrades-in-arms and faced her, eyeing each other as if to decide who should speak first.

Very rarely was she brought like this into Father's domain unless it was serious. Their unsmiling faces indicated a very grave situation indeed.

She waited.

Father's meerschaum pipe balanced on a ceramic plate near the edge of his desk. She saw the pipe infrequently as it was generally enjoyed with other men or privately as a relaxing diversion. The sweet-smelling scent of tobacco often lingered long after her father had benefited from a smoke, and she associated its aromatic cloud with one of his strong embraces. Familial tranquility.

Right now there were no feelings of peace in either man's presence.

Father looked her firmly in the eyes and went straight to the point. "Abigail is not who she pretends to be. She's known for harming others."

"Whatever can you mean?" Her voice squeaked.

"I'm afraid we have damaging evidence to prove the girl's maliciousness."

Clare leaned on her palms into the desktop and the pipe rattled. "Why haven't you told me this before?" Bile rose in her throat.

"We didn't want to make any accusations unless we had further evidence. You know I always try and give others the benefit of the doubt."

James said, "We've just had confirmation from Doctor Willard only a few moments ago. Results from the apothecary were the final verification of our suspicions. There was arsenic in the tea Grace drank. It must have been a smaller dosage than she gave your father as she's recovered sooner."

"Arsenic?" She swallowed hard. If what Father and James were saying were true, could the maid be responsible for his and Grace's malady? The thought of anyone dying because of her stubbornness was more than she could bear. Anger shifted into anguish. She brushed tears away with the back of her hand and tightened her jaw. "You had no right to hide all these details from me."

Father's eyes narrowed. "How dare you presume to dictate what rights I have or do not have in this house?"

Clare flinched. Like the rarity of viewing his pipe, she rarely saw her father this furious.

Father's bristled demeanor settled. "Do you realize how unreasonable you've been? Would you have listened? How many times has one of us tried to say something and you'd get defensive?" He exhaled a long breath as if to release his pent up anger and spoke evenly, controlled, "Granted I should have fired the girl straight away. Suffered the consequences of your ire for a few days. In hindsight it would have thwarted her intentions towards this household. I bear full responsibility."

A ball of emotional twine twisted in Clare's stomach. She felt sick; infuriated at the deceit of someone she had trusted. If only she'd listened to everyone in the first place, this would have never happened. "Someone else could have taken ill. Like Grace did. Or worse…could have perished."

"It's not unusual to have arsenic in the

house." Her father came around the desk and rested on one corner, his arms crossed. "We use it for all kinds of treatments. Even Doctor Willard prescribes it on an individual basis. The crime here is having a servant use it to make others ill."

"Has she done this before?" Lightheaded, Clare sat on the chair. Hadn't she validated Abigail's potential to everyone in the house? Now she was discovering the maid's treachery. Her deviousness.

Father reached around his back and lifted a stack of papers and pulled out a single sheaf. "James alerted me to a problem when he'd taken over my duties. Apparently another landowner had Abigail in their employment. They heard she had been hired by our family and sent a message of concern, but no specific details."

James came around the desk. "Mister Barnsley at Sunflower Cottage, you know, the man Doctor Willard had treated for gout, shared with the doctor rumors he'd heard about Abigail as well."

"I was beginning to have my own misgivings. Last night when I went into the kitchen she was hiding something. Then told me a lie."

"Apparently she's also been threatening our staff," James added.

"What?" Clare jumped as if hot tea had spilled all over her. This was beyond belief. How could she have been so blind? It was one thing to lose eyesight. It was another thing entirely to lose sight of truth.

"Their minds, not their bodies."

"Whatever do you mean?"

Her father placed the paper on top of the stack, the harshness gone from his tone. "Everett finally confessed to me, earlier, before everyone had woken, how Abigail had been abusing the staff with threats. She'd gathered evidence about each and had been blackmailing them with the details. She even bragged about sending a letter to the doctor saying I was getting better. If the servants tried to speak up, she would threaten to expose their pasts.

"She undermined them at every possible opportunity. Everett discovered Abigail even changed the Longcase clock to make me think he was being slack in his duties. It turned out another servant had observed her but was afraid to say. Because of Everett's consistent reliability, I knew better than to think wrongly of him.

"Plus, the girl had the audacity to defy me whenever I asked her to do something. We're telling you all of this right now because we wanted you to be aware the doctor alerted the authorities. They should be here any moment. We didn't say anything in the dining room as we didn't want Abigail to become suspicious and try to leave."

Clare turned away and whispered, "In

her defense, there's one thing I can say about her behavior."

"You mean you'll defend her even after this? Even I don't have that kind of solicitude," Father's anger rekindled, as she turned back.

"She knew I was going to drink the tea."

"And?"

"Abigail intentionally spilled it. She told me time and again she would do anything for me. I believe she would've never let me consume the tea."

Her father's eyes and tone softened. "I suppose you're right. She knew you had been the one person who defended her."

"Please forgive me, James, for not listening to your wise counsel. Father, I'm very sorry. I bear the responsibility for you getting ill."

"You mustn't take the blame for someone else's evil doings."

"Can you both forgive me?"

They nodded.

"I must go and apologize to Grace. She tried to warn me about Abigail's behavior towards Michael. I wouldn't believe her either. Plus the staff. I owe them an apology as well. I could tell they were overworked and unhappy."

Clare reached out to hug her father. The warm scent of his tobacco filled her nostrils, and she inhaled deeply. Familial comfort. His reassurance and James warm hand on her back were all she needed to be reminded of the gift of forgiveness and overflowing love.

Would she ever learn? Would she ever awake with the same understanding of people as her father? Maybe someday. But for now, she would embrace those who loved and accepted her without question.

Chapter Forty-nine

Sounds of scuffling feet, running and slamming of doors echoed in the corridor. Fredrick pulled from Clare's embrace and the three rushed into the foyer.

Elizabeth peered out of the dining room.

"What's going on?" Fredrick asked.

"Abigail's gone. No one can locate her."

"What?" He yanked the cord inside his office.

Everett appeared as if by magic.

"Where's Abigail?"

"I'm not certain." His manservant was flushed and breathless. "I was trying to keep my eye on her like you asked. I'm sorry, sir, I can't seem to find her."

"This isn't your fault. She's a sly one."

"Once you, Miss Clare and Master James left the dining room, she helped Miss Grace for a minute. Then followed after you. I thought perhaps she had forgotten to tell Miss Clare something. I watched her from the dining room to be sure she didn't leave the house."

"What happened next?"

"She stopped there." Everett nodded in the direction of Fredrick's office. "Then waited two or three minutes, turned and ran downstairs."

"She must have overheard us."

"I followed her to the kitchen thinking she'd be there, but she was already gone. The last anyone saw of her was upstairs in the maid's section coming out of her room with a bag."

Loud knocks on the front door made the entourage in the foyer halt in place.

Fredrick took charge. "Please open the door, Everett."

His firm tone jolted the others from their motionless stance. A renewed frenzy of activity started again as servants entered and exited from the parlor, the dining room and up and down the stairs in pursuit of the maid.

When the manservant opened the front door, Doctor Willard and Sam lingered on the threshold.

Three horses and their riders galloped down the lane towards the house.

The doctor said, "I went for Sam straight away after I broke the news of the tea. I thought we could use his help."

Horses' energetic hoofs kicked up gravel

as the authorities rode towards the entrance.

"Good morning, Master Shaw." Ely's constable and two fellow officers dismounted.

"Good morning, Mister Geoffrey. Thank you for coming." Fredrick had met the man when James had been in prison. He'd been extremely helpful in getting James released. "Everyone, please, come in."

"Thank you for your kindness." The constable removed his cap and exposed thick, grey eyebrows and a large protruding nose. His ears flapped out as if being released from the hat's clutch. Perspiring energy exuded from him.

The gaggle of men circled around the large table, the two officers holding their official caps under their arms. Doctor Willard and Sam joined them.

"Where's the girl?" Mister Geoffrey asked while standing at attention.

"We aren't sure. The last sighting, she was taking some personal belongings out of her room."

"You two men, circle the estate." Geoffrey directed his officers.

Both men tossed on their caps and hurried out.

"I'll go back to the stables and see if she's hiding there," Sam offered.

Fredrick motioned to James. "Perhaps you and the constable can check downstairs and around the sleeping quarters."

"Of course."

"Where's Grace?" Doctor Willard asked. "I wanted to be sure the effects of the arsenic have worn off entirely."

"She's in the dining room with Michael."

With everyone's dismissal, the foyer grew silent.

A slight whimpering came from a corner under the stairway.

"Why are you crying?" Fredrick joined Clare in the enclave, hands on hips. This young woman could bring out the best and worse in him at times.

"How can I forgive myself for what's happened?"

Right now she struck a cord of frustration with her self-disparagement. He checked his response. Anger wouldn't make the situation resolve itself. "You've learned a hard lesson. There's no denying it's been a difficult time."

She leaned her head on his shoulder. "I know I should be out with the others trying to find the miserable girl."

Fredrick circled an arm around her shoulder and the worst of his anger was replaced by the deep well of his love. "If she's still on the estate, one of them will catch her."

"I just don't want to face her." Clare's shoulders heaved with grief. "She's hurt those I love the most."

Fredrick waited for Clare to regain

composure. Who was he to deny his daughter time to lament? There were too many occasions a stiff upper lip was expected, dictated as the proper response in dealing with heartbreak. He whispered, "What else's bothering you?"

She shook her head and gazed at him with those large ebony eyes that had pierced his soul when she'd been a child and wept. Parents desired to shield their children. When they became adults there was no longer the ability to protect them.

"Jean. I miss her. I realize now I was trying to replace her as quickly as I could so I wouldn't feel the emptiness in here." She jabbed her chest. "I thought Abigail could be that person."

Fredrick choked. "I miss Jean, too. When we lose someone we love, it's as if all the mourning over our lifetime returns. Each loss seems to become greater than the last. What you're feeling is perfectly understandable."

"While I was focusing on defending Abigail and wanting her to fill a void, I forgot you and Sam."

"We share in our suffering. All of us. Jesus said we would share in His too. It's part of life but it doesn't have to define who we become. Suffering sanctifies."

"You're such a wise man, Father."

"My dear girl, I only speak from my own mistakes and the lessons I've learned."

"Let's go into the dining room, shall we, and see how Grace is getting on? We'll wait there until we hear from the others."

+ + +

"I'm afraid she's nowhere to be found." James entered the dining room. "The constable and his men searched the grounds and have headed back to Ely for the time being. There's nothing left for them to do here."

"Where ever she's gone, I pray she doesn't harm anyone else." Clare sat between Grace and Elizabeth at the table.

Michael stood behind Grace's chair, resting his hands on her shoulders.

"We've done what we can for the time being," the doctor said.

"Let's put aside the disruption. We have cause for celebration. Let's not allow Abigail to destroy yet another part of our lives by ruining this wonderful occasion. Michael has asked Grace to be his wife. I for one want to rejoice in their union," Fredrick lifted a water glass as in a mock salute.

"Here. Here." Everyone shouted and raised a glass.

Grace beamed and Michael blushed.

Clare laughed generously and Elizabeth made her way over to Fredrick.

If James had anything to say about it, he and Fredrick wouldn't allow anyone to break the family bond no matter how hard they might try.

Chapter Fifty

Patrick Tripp traipsed Willow Field's flagstone kitchen floor, stopped and listened.

Activities of cooking, chatter of Phoebe directing the servants comings and goings, and Sara gleefully pounding a tiny lump of dough on the center table filled his senses with overflowing joy.

Daniel, snuggled in a cot by the fireplace slept peacefully in spite of the noise. The baby's woolen blanket slid gently, up and down, up and down with each inhale and exhale. If he could, he'd pause this exact moment and never allow the sands of time to steal its pleasure.

Sara, concentration engraved across her tiny features, glanced up.

"What are you creating, little one?" He chuckled as he sat down beside her.

She released a long sigh of indignation that she had to explain. "Dada. It's brea." Added another small punch to the dough.

"Oh, bread for our tea, is it?"

She shook her head and returned to the lump, forming a ball appearing more like a clump of overused clay than a loaf to be served.

"Isn't she doing a marvelous job?" Phoebe laid a gentle hand on his shoulder.

His wife's touch was aloe on a burn. The pain he had endured was still undergoing a healing process, but each day the hurt had less and less control over his heart.

He covered her hand with his. "Well, she's had an excellent teacher."

She leaned over and kissed his cheek.

Another layer of aloe. More of the ache gradually vanishing.

Phoebe pointed at the sizable window facing the back garden. "Who do you suppose that is?" The noise in the kitchen ceased. "It looked like Clare's maid going past."

Patrick quickly rose and opened the door. The girl had vanished. "Why would she come here?"

"I've no idea but perhaps we should contact the Shaws."

"Were you absolutely certain it was her?"

"I do believe it was, but I could be mistaken. She passed by so quickly." Phoebe turned to the servant girls. "Were any of you expecting a visit from Abigail, Mistress Clare's maid?"

The girls shook their heads. "No, miss."

"It's a clear day, I'll take one the horses for a ride and see if she's anywhere around the estate. If not, I'll go to Bethel Manor and confirm she's there and we were mistaken. Whoever it was needs to be found. We don't want strangers loitering around."

"Are you fine going to see James and Fredrick?"

Patrick sensed a hesitation in Phoebe's voice.

"Yes. That's behind me, behind us now. We need to move ahead with our lives."

Phoebe drew near and laid a hand on his chest. "I'm pleased to hear it. I would like to meet with Clare and the children if the opportunity arises in the future. I didn't want to give you cause for concern though."

"Trust is like building a home. One brick must be laid for the rest to fit securely. We've begun to relay the foundation of our marriage. You must have freedom to enjoy your friends without worrying about me."

"Thank you." Phoebe whispered. "I want to grow old with you."

"And I with you." He smiled and chuckled. "Grow so old together we won't recognize each other by the end."

Patrick's longing surged upward from deep within his soul. Places he never knew existed. A flicker of hope burst into a fire of passion and he drew her into his arms securely and kissed her with tense hunger. His internal pain shattered into a million fragments and love filled the deep, empty crevices.

Sara said, "Silly Mummy. Dada."

Three of the girl servants giggled as they passed cleaned dishes along the counter and the last servant stacked the plates in a cupboard.

They pulled apart. Phoebe kept her eyes lowered.

"I'll return as quickly as possible." Patrick pecked the top of Sara's head. "You be a good girl and finish what you're working on. We'll enjoy some of your bread on my return."

Sara nodded, riveted by the lump once more.

Patrick made his way to the stables, chose the youngest and sturdiest of the mares, vaulted onto her back and clicked his tongue.

After checking outbuildings and searching the part of the estate stretching east and south, Patrick headed towards Bethel Manor. Whoever had bounded past the kitchen window seemed to be long gone.

+ + +

James secured the straps on the saddle and mounted Sentra. Abigail had to be somewhere nearby. He tugged left on the reins and steered the horse away from the stable yard.

Out the pillared gates, through the bare chestnut tree brigade lining the entrance and he was finally able to allow the animal to stretch her legs into a full gallop.

Late February brought with it the unpredictable warmer days and this afternoon was disguised with spring like qualities. He wouldn't be lulled into thinking the lack of snow, warmer air and green shoots meant they'd turned the corner on winter. Every year the change was deceitful and landowners could be duped into planting too soon. Fredrick was no fool and had a natural ability to know when the season was ripe for sowing.

Up ahead another horse and rider quickly approached.

James sat upright and yanked the reins.

Patrick. Riding with the haste as if on a mission. Had he failed to get over the anger and returned to point fingers of accusations again? Would the man never realize how much his wife loved him? How much James loved Clare?

Right now his focus was finding Abigail. Clare had no idea he'd left on this expedition. He wasn't going to let the girl hurt another soul. And he wasn't about to let Patrick stop him from accomplishing his task.

Patrick galloped up to him and dropped to the ground. "There you are. I was just coming to see you. We need to talk."

Chapter Fifty-one

"Thank you for making us aware of Abigail's whereabouts." James shook Patrick's hand and brought him up to date on the maid's horrendous misdeeds.

It's the least I could do." Patrick's self-assured attitude and warm smile had returned. A sure sign there was hope for their friendship. "We were totally unaware of her behavior."

"Would you like to come with me to the house and inform the family? We can also get word to the authorities."

"I'd be happy to join you. She needs to be found, taken to Ely and prosecuted."

James shuddered at the thought. No one should be subjected to that dismal gaol no matter the seriousness of the crime. "I suppose that's the only option."

James led the journey back to Bethel, and quiet camaraderie accompanied him and Patrick.

Fredrick welcomed them on the manor's threshold. "Gentlemen, I saw your approach from my office. What's the news?"

James dropped from his horse. "We believe Abigail's at Willow Field. Although Patrick searched and couldn't find her, we think it's prudent to send the authorities and double check."

"Good idea." Fredrick rang the bell for Everett. "Have word sent to Ely's constabulary. At once."

"Yes, sir."

"Won't you join us for a chat before heading home, Patrick?" James looked up at his friend. It was good when men could reconcile without the need to rehash an incident over and over as women seemed prone to do.

"I'd like that." Patrick dismounted and handed his reins to a young stable hand.

The men made their way to the smoking room.

Fredrick had recently been enjoying his pipe as ringlets of smoke curled from its bowl.

"Would you care for a smoke?"

Patrick and James shook their heads.

"Please sit." Fredrick sat in an overstuffed family heirloom chair, its leather cushion worn from centuries of use. "You won't mind if I indulge?"

"Of course not."

"You've had a terrible time of it recently."

Patrick sat.

James hovered by the fireplace.

"It's been dreadful how this girl was so conniving and created dissension within the staff, but we're over her shenanigans. We've plenty of wonderful events to tell you about." As Fredrick sucked gently on the tip of the pipe's mouthpiece, vapors hovered close to the ceiling as if a cloud hung inside.

"Really? I can't wait to hear. Phoebe will be excited to know about them as well."

"First off, Grace is engaged to Michael."

Patrick reclined in his chair and stretched out his legs. "That *is* indeed great news. I'm so pleased for her. For them."

"What else is there to share?" James asked, smiling.

"There's a big party being planned. Of course the entire Tripp family is welcome. We wouldn't want any of you to miss out on the merriment. Clare wants everyone to come in costumes and masks, of course. From what I understand, there'll be a variety of games plus musicians from the village."

"We'd love to attend. Any excuse for ladies to dress up. Phoebe is no exception."

"Absolutely."

"Plus a search is on for a new housemaid. We've sat down as a family with Sam and asked his advice. We will be scheduling interviews and he's agreed to assist in the decision. In the meantime, several maids have joined together and are making the kitchen manageable. Once that dreadful girl was out of the picture, it was like dead flowers had been watered, and the servants are flourishing and blooming again."

"You appear relaxed and more like yourself," Patrick added.

"It's been a challenging couple of months there's no denying it."

Patrick looked down. "I added to your sorrow and deeply regret the part I played."

Fredrick leaned back, released a small billow from his mouth and smiled. "There's always bound to be disruptions among those we love."

"That's very kind of you to say, thank you."

"What seems to be the matter, James? You've been fidgeting since you came in." Fredrick held his pipe at the base of the bowl, waiting to take another puff.

"It seems there's other news to share." James scratched his cheek. How should he tell these men?

"Spit it out, man."

"I'm not sure I should be the one to say."

"Is everything fine with Clare?"

"Well, that's just it. I'm not sure."

Fredrick laid the pipe on the tray beside his chair. "What's wrong, James?"

"It seems I'm going to be a father again."

"What?" Both men jumped and clapped James on the back.

"Why didn't you say so? Are you certain? Is Clare all right?" Fredrick headed towards the door and opened it.

Clare and Elizabeth waited in the foyer and turned towards them.

Fredrick paused. James clapped his back. "Why don't you go and congratulate your daughter."

Clare's father shifted towards her a step. "My dearest girl… you should be in bed after the horrible ordeal you had with your last pregnancy." He took his daughter's elbow and began to gently guide her towards the stairwell."

She shrugged his hand away gently and giggled. "I do believe you might be overreacting. I'm pregnant, not dying. Even James didn't try to sequester me in my room." She hugged him. "I hope you're pleased."

"You know I am. But I'll be worried every moment. I'll send for the doctor and have him monitor you each day." Fredrick's face creased in thought.

James draped his arm around Clare. "We couldn't be happier. And, Patrick, I wanted to let you know as long as you were here with us."

Patrick reached out a hand and they shook. "I'm very pleased for each of you and can't wait to share every tidbit of news with Phoebe. It's very exciting to say the least."

"And the party. Don't forget the party."

"I wouldn't dream of it." Patrick accepted his coat and hat.

"Before you go," Elizabeth murmured.

The group stopped chattering and glanced at her.

"Now I feel quite conspicuous." She toyed with the lacey edge of a handkerchief.

"What's the matter, my dear?"

"It's just that everyone's sharing their surprises. I have one to disclose as well."

"You do?" Fredrick approached her with tentative steps.

The foyer became silent as a crypt.

Everyone waited.

"It seems Clare is not the only one with child. Surprise, Fredrick Shaw, you are going to become a father and grandfather at the same time. I do hope you aren't disappointed."

"Disappointed?" Fredrick grabbed her by the waist, lifted her slightly off the floor and placed her gingerly back in place. "I'm in love and you're with child. Now I know how Abraham must have felt."

He pulled her close, threw back his head and laughed until tears coursed down his face.

"I'm the happiest man in the whole world."

Meet the Author

Beatrice Fishback, originally from upstate New York, lived in the East Anglian area of Great Britain for over twenty years. She and her husband have traveled extensively in the United Kingdom and throughout Europe, and have spoken to audiences worldwide.

They have two children and two grandchildren.

Currently, they divide their time between North Carolina and England.

Her two great loves are dark chocolate and a good natter with a friend.

Readers can visit Bea's website at beasattitudes.net, and find her on Facebook @beasattitudes.

Made in the USA
Columbia, SC
08 October 2018